Accidental
DETECTIVES

Legend
OF THE
Gilded Saber

SIGMUND BROUWER

BETHANYHOUSE
MINNEAPOLIS, MINNESOTA

Legend of the Gilded Saber
Copyright © 2002
Sigmund Brouwer

Cover illustration by Chris Ellison
Cover design by Lookout Design Group, Inc.

Published by Bethany House Publishers
A Ministry of Bethany Fellowship International
11400 Hampshire Avenue South
Bloomington, Minnesota 55438
www.bethanyhouse.com

Printed in the United States of America by
Bethany Press International, Bloomington, Minnesota 55438

Library of Congress Cataloging-in-Publication Data

Brouwer, Sigmund, 1959-
    Legend of the gilded saber / by Sigmund Brouwer.
        p. cm. —(Accidental detectives)
    Summary: Ricky and friends attempt to solve the mystery of a museum theft in Charleston, South Carolina.
    ISBN 0–7642–2566–9
    [1. Mystery and detective stories. 2. Charleston (S.C.)—Fiction. 3. Stealing—Fiction. 4. Christian life—Fiction.] I. Title. II. Series: Brouwer, Sigmund, 1959- . Accidental detectives.
    PZ7.B79984Lg   2002
    [Fic]—dc21   2002010720

(5) 11-07

Legend
OF THE
Gilded Saber

50

Children's Books by
Sigmund Brouwer

THE ACCIDENTAL DETECTIVES

The Volcano of Doom
The Disappearing Jewel of Madagascar
Legend of the Gilded Saber
Tyrant of the Badlands

WATCH OUT FOR JOEL

Bad Bug Blues
Long Shot

SIGMUND BROUWER is the award-winning author of scores of books. He speaks to kids around the continent in an effort to instill good reading and writing habits in the next generation. Sigmund and his wife, Cindy Morgan, divide their time between Tennessee and Alberta, Canada.

For Olivia
and the sunshine you bring
into this world

CHAPTER 1

"How far do you think I could get one of these Cheetos up Ralphy's nose?" I whispered to my friend Mike Andrews.

Mike's uncle, a stockbroker named Theodore Emmett, had paid our travel expenses to bring the three of us and our friend Lisa Higgins to Charleston, South Carolina. The deal was simple. If the four of us agreed to be caddies at a historically reenacted golf tournament, we could have the rest of a week of vacation in Charleston.

Lisa was outside somewhere, talking to the golfer she would be a caddy for.

Mike and I were alone with Ralphy Zee, who slept nearby in a chair in the men's locker room of the clubhouse at the golf course. As I spoke to Mike, I munched from a bag of Cheetos—those narrow, long, cheese-flavored snacks. It wasn't much for breakfast, but at least it was something.

"Cheetos?" Mike stared at me as if I were crazy. Which was unfair. Of anyone I knew, Mike Andrews was the craziest. Red hair. Freckles.

Except for this morning, dressed in plaid knickers and a vested sweater like a caddy from the nineteenth century, he usually wore a wild-looking Hawaiian shirt and a New York Yankees ball cap. Even though he was only twelve, he had already managed to pack twenty years of pranks into his life. It was always Mike Andrews coming up with the wild ideas. "Up Ralphy's nose?"

"Sure." I held up a Cheeto. It would fit perfectly in a human nostril. "Listen to Ralphy snore. He's exhausted from the trip here."

The night before, thunderstorms had delayed our flight into Charleston by nearly eight hours. We had not landed until two in the morning. Theodore Emmett had sent a taxi for us because he'd lent his white Mercedes to his son, Devon. Between picking up our luggage and taking the taxi, it had been another hour before we reached Mike's uncle's house. And now it was seven in the morning, barely four hours later, and there were about fifteen minutes before we were called to the tee box to carry golf clubs for Mr. Emmett, his business partner, and the president and vice-president of the country club.

"But Cheetos up his nose *here*?" he whispered back. Mike wasn't whispering because he was afraid of waking Ralphy. He was afraid one of the members of the club might overhear us. When we'd told the taxi driver last night about the golf tournament, he'd whistled and let us know it cost more to join this country club than most people made in five years.

"This is . . . this is . . ." Mike lifted his arms, gesturing to our surroundings, still whispering as if afraid of offending any of the wealthy members of the club.

The lockers were not cheap metal, like the ones at our school gym. These lockers were made of stained walnut, and each locker had an engraved nameplate with a member's name. The floor was lush carpet. Massive old paintings filled the walls. At the back of the locker room was a shower area with a whirlpool and a steam room. We sat in an area with leather-covered reclining chairs in front of a big-screen television.

"This is the snobbiest place we've ever been?" I finished for Mike.

"Exactly," he said in hushed tones. "Not even *I* would put a Cheeto up Ralphy's nose here. I'm not even sure we're allowed in this area."

"You're just jealous because I thought of it first."

"Hah," he said. "I'm just not crazy enough to try. Even if we were back in Jamesville. You know what Ralphy is like. One little touch on his nose, and he'll jump through the roof."

"And I also know that while you and I slept on the airplane, he was so scared he couldn't even look out the window. And you can bet he hardly got any sleep the night before because he was so worried about flying. And last night, after getting in late, he probably stayed awake most of the night worrying about doing something wrong at this golf tournament. Which means he's only had a couple hours of sleep in the last two nights. Now he's so dead to the world, I'm pretty sure I could get a Cheeto halfway up each nostril."

I could see Mike thinking that through. "No way," he

finally said. "This is still Ralphy we're talking about."

I could tell Mike was hooked. I hoped Ralphy wouldn't smile and give it away that he wasn't sleeping after all.

"Yes way," I said. I pretended to give this situation some more thought myself. But it was just pretense. Mike is usually the one playing pranks on Ralphy or me. In fact, on the last day of school, he'd squirted quick-drying superglue onto the seat of my chair just before I sat at my desk. Five minutes later, when I'd tried to stand to leave for school assembly, I'd ripped my pants. And this was only two days after squirting the same superglue into Ralphy's baseball cap. Now, three weeks into summer vacation, Ralphy's hair still had big patches missing from where he'd been forced to pull the hat loose.

"Tell you what," I continued to Mike. "If Ralphy wakes up, I'll cut your lawn all summer when we get to Jamesville. But if I manage to get one Cheeto halfway up each nostril, you cut my lawn all summer."

"I don't know," Mike said. "Uncle Ted says this place is very snooty and—"

"Chicken?"

Mike straightened and glared at me. "Not a chance."

I stuck my hand out. "We've got a deal?"

He shook on it.

I hid a smile. There was no way I could lose. Ralphy and I had already arranged this the night before. Ralphy was going to pretend to sleep as long as it took for me to get both Cheetos in his nose. We'd have our revenge on Mike. Not a single thing could go wrong.

Except that just as I managed to shove the second

Cheeto up Ralphy's second nostril, a loud, angry voice interrupted us.

"What are you boys doing in this area of the men's locker room?!"

Mike and I spun around to see a man named Jonathan Wentsworth, the president of the country club. I knew this because Mr. Emmett had pointed him out to us the moment we got to the country club—and had warned us to be on our best behavior around him.

Wentsworth was a big man, wearing old-style golf clothes. He had a huge bald head and a walrus mustache. And a face instantly red with anger.

"What are you boys doing here?" he demanded again. "Caddies are not permitted here!"

I kept myself between the president and Ralphy, who was still reclining in the leather chair. I didn't think Wentsworth would be amused to see Cheetos up Ralphy's nose.

"Sir," I said, "we knew we weren't supposed to be ready for a few minutes. We just thought—"

"You don't think around here," Wentsworth said. "You follow the rules. Who are your parents? I'll have to have a talk with them."

"We're from out of town," Mike explained. "My uncle invited us to help him with this tournament for your club."

"Uncle? We have golfers coming in from all over the world for this. Don't expect me to know who your uncle is."

"Ted Emmett," Mike said. Mr. Emmett was also an

amateur historian and the person who ran this tournament. "He's here to—"

"Theodore Emmett." Wentsworth sniffed with disdain. "So I suppose that means you're the caddies he's picked out for us."

"Yes, sir," Mike said.

Wentsworth's frown deepened. "Why isn't that young man behind you out of his chair and standing with respect for his elders?"

I stepped aside, hoping that Ralphy had managed to pull the Cheetos out of his nose.

"Ralphy?" I said quietly.

Ralphy jumped to his feet and joined Mike and me, facing Wentsworth. I took a quick glance at Ralphy's face and sighed with relief. No Cheetos. I couldn't imagine how much more yelling we would have faced with orange Cheetos sticking out of Ralphy's nose like chopsticks.

I guess, though, Wentsworth still didn't approve of Ralphy's appearance. Ralphy's mouse-brown hair stuck straight up. He was small, and his clothing hung loose on him. He had a skinny face that sometimes twitched with nervousness.

"Straighten up," Wentsworth told Ralphy. "Make yourself presentable."

Ralphy ran his fingers through his hair, but it didn't help.

Wentsworth sighed. "Out to the tee box immediately," he ordered. "And don't let me catch you in here again. I don't care how important Ted Emmett is to the historical society; if any of you misbehave again, all of you will be gone."

"Yes, sir," I said.

"Yes, sir," Mike said.

But Wentsworth didn't reply. He had already walked away, expecting us to follow.

Ralphy didn't say anything, either.

That's when I noticed the tears running out of his eyes and a trickle of orange running onto his upper lip from each nostril.

Which gave me a bad feeling about exactly where the Cheetos had gone . . . and still were.

CHAPTER 2

It was a beautiful, cloudless July day. Hot. And humid with the heavy air that hung over the coast of South Carolina.

To our right was the magnificent clubhouse, three stories tall with large glass windows that overlooked the fairways. To our left was a large pond. And at our sides were the old-fashioned golf bags we were about to carry for eighteen holes. The golf bags contained mashie niblicks and all the other ancient wood-shafted clubs that were actually used over a hundred years earlier. My thoughts, however, were not on the golf course or the golf tournament that required our presence as caddies.

"Let me see if I understood you correctly," I said in a low voice to Ralphy. "It was Mike?"

Since Wentsworth had made us immediately follow him outside to the first tee box, then made us wait here as he went back to the clubhouse to find his playing partners, Ralphy had not even had time to get some tissue.

"He shoved them up my nose!" When Ralphy was excited or angry his voice became a high squeak. Like now. But it had also become a very nasal-sounding high squeak. Cheetos in the nose do that to people.

"You shoved them up his nose?" I said to Mike.

"Hey," Mike protested. "When Wentsworth stomped in, what else could I do?"

"Could have let me pull them out," Ralphy said. A constant stream of orange ran out of his nose. He wiped it away with his shirt sleeve, which left an orange stain on the sleeve. I doubted Wentsworth would like that; just Ralphy's luck to be his caddy.

"You couldn't have pulled them out," Mike said. "You were asleep."

I shook my head at Ralphy so that he wouldn't tell Mike he'd actually been awake the whole time. Ralphy and I needed to keep that secret.

"Well, then," I said quickly to Mike, "*you* could have pulled them out instead of mashing them in."

"Pull Cheetos out of his nose?" Mike made a face. "Then I would have had to hold them and hide them in my hand. Slimy, orange, and gross. You think I wanted that?"

Ralphy wiped away more of the orange stream from his upper lip. "And you think I wanted them jammed almost into my brain?"

Ralphy's eyes kept watering, which explained why stuff kept running from his nose. "Come on," he moaned. "I can't walk around all day like this. We have to do something."

"How about this," Mike said. He reached over and used

his thumb and forefinger to squeeze Ralphy's nose, hard.

"Waaaah!" Ralphy said. "What'd you do that for?"

"Shhh!" I said. "Any second they'll be back out."

As if to confirm, a voice came over the loudspeaker. "For the seven-fifteen tee time, Wentsworth, Mandily, Emmett, and Stang."

"Give your head a shake," Mike told Ralphy.

"Give your own head a shake," Ralphy said, really mad now. "First you shove Cheetos up my nose. Then you mash them!"

"No, really," Mike answered. "Give your head a shake. The reason I squeezed your nose was to break the Cheetos into little pieces."

Ralphy squinted in suspicion.

"Come on," Mike said. "Our golfers just got paged. Better get that stuff out of your nose before they get here."

Ralphy shook his head. Orange crumbs trickled from his nose down into the grass at his feet. He shook harder. More crumbs fell out.

"Great work," I said to Mike. "But you still owe me."

"Huh?"

"I got those Cheetos up his nose before he woke," I said. "You'll have to cut my lawn all summer."

"But . . ." Mike hesitated. There was nothing he could say. He would have to cut the lawn.

"But nothing." I grinned in triumph.

"Guys!" Ralphy spoke again. Still with a nasal tone. "The rest are still stuck up there."

"Huh?" Mike was still thinking about cutting my lawn. He didn't understand what Ralphy meant.

"The Cheetos." Ralphy's eyes still streamed water. Orange goo still came out of his nose. "All you did was break off the bottom half of each. I can still feel them way up there. And I think they're too soggy to move."

"Blow," Mike said.

"Huh?"

"Press one finger against one nostril," Mike said with great patience, "and blow hard to clear the other. Then do the other side. Just make sure you point your nose away from us."

"But—" Ralphy began.

"Enough talk," Wentsworth barked as he and two other men approached the tee box. "Caddies should be seen, not heard. And my caddy must set the example."

All three of them wore knickers and old-fashioned caps. The whole point of this golf tournament was to play with equipment and clothing that would have been used in the late 1800s.

Behind Wentsworth, the second man was skinny and in his mid-fifties. I only knew his name because I would be caddying for him. Thomas Stang, the stockbroker who was Ted Emmett's business partner. He'd picked all of us up in his black Lincoln Navigator an hour earlier.

With Ralphy caddying for Jonathan Wentsworth, and me the caddy for Thomas Stang, that left Mike as caddy for the third man. Theodore Emmett, Mike's uncle. He insisted that we call him Ted. Ted, who was in his late forties, had a hollow, worn face, and constantly smoked. Like now. He sucked on a cigarette, flicked it into a bush, and winked at the three of us, as if telling us to ignore the stuffiness of Jonathan Wentsworth.

Seconds later Lisa Higgins followed with a fourth man, Jonathan Mandily, who had a completely bald head. Lisa smiled at us. I managed to fake a smile back.

"Ready, gentlemen?" Wentsworth said to the other three.

Each nodded. Each withdrew a club from the golf bags that Mike, Lisa, and I held balanced beside us.

Not Wentsworth. He barked another order at Ralphy and made Ralphy pull out a club to give to him.

Wentsworth watched as Tom Stang hit a drive first. The ball didn't go far. But it was what was called a machined gutta, a ball from the 1890s, not anything like a modern golf ball for distance. Plus it was hit by a club with a wooden shaft instead of steel or graphite.

Then Mike's uncle Ted hit his drive. It went down the middle and a little farther than Stang's drive.

Finally it was Jonathan Wentsworth's turn. He walked to the tee box and began to ready himself with great ceremony. He stepped away from his ball a few times. He looked down the fairway. At the ball. At the fairway. Thirty seconds later he still had not yet swung. I could tell this was going to be a long day.

Then, just as he began to draw his club back to hit the ball, Ralphy sneezed. Loudly.

Wentsworth stepped away from the golf ball and glared at Ralphy. "Another interruption like that, young man, and I'll send you packing."

"Yes, sir," Ralphy said, his voice filled with misery. Not a nasal-sounding misery, just normal misery. His sneeze must have cleared his nostrils of the remaining pieces of Cheetos.

Wentsworth began to address the ball again.

Mike elbowed me and pointed. At a slimy piece of Cheeto that clung to Wentsworth's golf ball like a dead orange caterpillar.

Wentsworth noticed it, too.

"What on earth is that?" Wentsworth exploded. He leaned down to peer at it more closely.

I looked at Ralphy. There was an orange trail down his chin.

I looked at Wentsworth, who had lifted the slimy Cheeto to examine it closer to his eyes. He squinted at it.

I looked at Mike, who was gritting his jaws to keep from laughing.

Lisa, dark-haired and blue-eyed, had a suspicious look on her face, as if she knew Mike and I were up to something but couldn't figure out what.

I looked at Tom Stang and Ted Emmett, who were giving each other puzzled glances.

"I believe it's dead," Wentsworth pronounced. "But where did it come from? I need to talk to the greenskeeper about this. The members will be outraged if some type of orange caterpillar decides to attack our shrubbery."

He put his hands on his hips to survey the tree above the tee box, as if perhaps the offending insect had dropped from a branch.

"Oh, man," Mike said quietly between his tight jaws as Wentsworth marched around looking for more caterpillars. "I have to laugh so bad, I think I need diapers."

Me too. I knew if either of us started to laugh, we'd never stop. Which would get us kicked out of the tournament for certain. So I put one of my knuckles in my mouth and bit as hard as I could, hoping it would prevent any giggles.

"Hah!" Wentsworth proclaimed, stooping to reach something on the grass. "Another!"

He'd found the second Cheeto from Ralphy's nose and picked it up.

"Most peculiar," he said to the others. He sniffed it. "Dead, just like the first. And rather slippery, too."

Just as I was about to drop to my knees and howl with laughter at Wentsworth, two policemen in uniform walked out of the clubhouse and toward the tee box. It was enough of a distraction to rescue me. That was the good news.

"Sorry to interrupt," the first one said as they got closer, "but we're looking for Ted Emmett."

That was the bad news. Thirty seconds later they arrested Mike's uncle right there. On the tee box. In front of the clubhouse.

With a television crew waiting on the street to film all of it.

CHAPTER 3

I stared in fascination at the old buildings lin-
ing both sides of the street. Mike and Ralphy and
Lisa and I were in a taxi, and we'd left the country
club twenty minutes earlier. The route had taken
us from the outskirts of Charleston to the historic
area on the southern peninsula.

The buildings were brick and stone, facing
sideways to the street, with long porches running
down the sides. Many of the buildings were pushed
right up to the street, with no yards or lawns. I'd
read about Charleston before leaving our home-
town of Jamesville, and I knew that many of the
buildings were hundreds of years old.

Charleston was one of the oldest cities in the
United States. It had been founded in 1670 and was
first named Charles Town, in honor of King
Charles II of England. Charleston had survived a
couple of wars—the War of Independence against
the British, and the Civil War. Plus it had survived
hurricanes and fires and earthquakes.

The southern peninsula itself was a piece of

land barely a mile wide, with the Ashley and Cooper Rivers on each side. It was only a few feet above sea level, and both of those rivers emptied a few miles away into the Atlantic.

Seeing the old city reminded me a lot of photographs of crowded European towns, until the taxi reached the very end of the peninsula. Here it was much different. A row of huge mansions faced the water.

"Wow," I said when the taxi stopped.

The four of us stepped out of the taxi and walked from the street up the sidewalk to the Emmett mansion.

"Wow," I said again, staring at the columns and the wide front porch. The mansion seemed like a smaller version of the White House in Washington, D.C. "This is something."

When we had arrived the night before, it had been too dark to really appreciate where we were staying. All I'd really seen was the hallway on my way to the guest room where I'd placed my luggage. We'd left for the golf course so early, I hadn't seen much more on my way out. Now, in the sunshine, I saw how big the place was. And how beautiful.

"Yeah," Lisa said. "Like from the movie *Gone With the Wind.*"

She was right. Large flowering bushes screened the porch railing. Vines climbed up the side of the house. The balconies were huge. The front of the mansion overlooked a park called White Point Gardens. Beyond that was the harbor where the Ashley and Cooper Rivers joined as they flowed out to the Atlantic Ocean. From where we stood, we could see the distant outline of Fort Sumter, an island where the first cannon shots of the Civil War were fired in 1861.

"Yeah," Mike said without enthusiasm. "Beautiful."

I didn't blame him for his depressed mood. I'd feel the same if I had just watched my uncle get escorted to a police cruiser in front of all the guests and members at the country club. Especially since we didn't know why he'd been arrested.

Mike flopped himself onto a large wicker chair on the porch.

Ralphy and Lisa and I found chairs beside him.

"So," I said to Mike, "what next?"

Mike stared over the lawn, at the street and the water beyond. "I don't know. I mean, we don't even have a key to get inside. And I sure don't feel like calling my mother and telling her that her brother's just been thrown in jail. Not with the other stuff going on in her life."

The other stuff was going on in Mike's life, too, but he hated to talk about it and pretended it didn't bother him. It was the troubles between his mother and his father. They were separated right now, and it was tough on Mike. I had hoped going to Charleston would take his mind off it, but now...

"It's got to be a mistake," Ralphy said. "There's nothing your uncle would do against the law, right? I mean, look at this place. It's not like he needs to steal anything. Not with his money. Right?"

Mike didn't answer.

A hummingbird buzzed past us and stopped to sip at a feeder hanging nearby.

"Right?" Ralphy repeated.

"I wish I could answer that," Mike said. "I hardly know him. He's always been too busy to visit and too busy for us to visit him. Then, out of the blue, he calls my mom and says he's sorry that they never get together and would it be all right for me to visit to make up for lost time."

Mike had told his uncle over the phone that he had three friends that he had promised to go to a summer camp with. Ralphy and Lisa and me. So his uncle had volunteered to bring us out as well. It helped that his uncle was an amateur historian and was in charge of running a historical golf tournament that needed some caddies. And by the size of the house Mike's uncle lived in, it sure seemed like he could afford the plane tickets.

"So all I really know about him," Mike continued, "is that he and his partner have a successful stockbroker business here in Charleston. That he bought this mansion because he's a historical preservationist. And that before his wife died, they had a son, who is now in his twenties."

"That would be me," a voice said from the open window behind us. "Come on in, and I'll tell you what I just learned from Dad's lawyer."

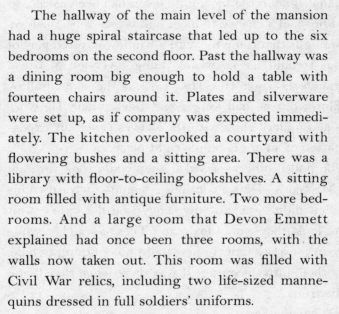

CHAPTER 4

The hallway of the main level of the mansion had a huge spiral staircase that led up to the six bedrooms on the second floor. Past the hallway was a dining room big enough to hold a table with fourteen chairs around it. Plates and silverware were set up, as if company was expected immediately. The kitchen overlooked a courtyard with flowering bushes and a sitting area. There was a library with floor-to-ceiling bookshelves. A sitting room filled with antique furniture. Two more bedrooms. And a large room that Devon Emmett explained had once been three rooms, with the walls now taken out. This room was filled with Civil War relics, including two life-sized mannequins dressed in full soldiers' uniforms.

This was the room where Devon led us after letting us into the mansion. We all sat on cane-backed chairs and waited for him to speak.

"So you're Mike," he said, nodding directly at Mike. "I recognize you from the pictures your mother sends every year on your birthday. Lousy way to meet, huh?"

Mike nodded. "I still can't believe it's actually happening. He didn't do anything wrong, right?"

"That's not the way it looks," Devon said. "An anonymous tip led the police here this morning just after Stang stopped by to pick all of you up."

Stang, of course, was Ted Emmett's business partner. There'd been plenty of room for all of us in his gigantic sports utility vehicle.

At that time in the morning Devon had been asleep, so we had not had a chance to meet him before this. Shadows from sunlight that came through a window covered part of him, but I could see he was a younger version of Uncle Ted, minus the cigarettes. His face was the same, hollow and skinny, but he had longer and thicker hair. He wore khakis and a black shirt with the sleeves rolled up, exposing a tattoo of an angel on his right bicep.

"The police officers asked if they could look through Dad's Mercedes," Devon continued, leaning forward on his chair, "but didn't explain why. They said if I didn't want them to look, they would leave an officer to watch it while they went for a warrant. I knew there was nothing to hide, so I let them into the garage. I was there when they found it in the trunk."

"It?" Mike asked.

Devon allowed himself a half smile. "It. The one possession in this world that Dad couldn't use his money to buy."

He ran his hands through his hair. "My dad collects pieces of history. This is his Civil War room. You haven't had a chance to see some of the upstairs rooms, but he has them grouped in themes. One room has golf stuff, centuries old. Which is why he arranges the yearly ancient golf tournament. Another room for tennis history. A third for things related to Charleston's marine history. All together, he has seven rooms with seven different themes. The house could be a museum. And of all his rooms, this is his favorite. The Civil War."

Devon stood and pointed at an empty glass case hanging on the wall like a picture frame. The long, narrow case was lined with velvet on the inside. It was empty.

"Dad has had that hanging there for years. He was determined to fill it with a saber that legend says General Sherman used to point at Atlanta as he gave the command to burn it to the ground. He left the case empty to remind him every day of his determination. Trouble was, the saber belonged to another private collector, who refused to sell it to him, even when Dad offered him a hundred thousand dollars. They'd been enemies a long time, ever since they'd both once proposed to the same woman, who said no to each of them and married someone else. In many ways, this part of Charleston is like a small village. People have long memories."

Mike coughed. "Funny, I thought I just heard you say a hundred thousand dollars. For a sword."

Devon smiled grimly. "I did. The handle was gilded with gold plating, but even so, at an auction it wouldn't be worth more than ten thousand dollars. But Dad absolutely hates it when he can't get his way. He was willing to pay ten times its worth to get it. The other private collector knew how much Dad wanted it, and in the end, because of their feud, managed to make sure Dad would never get his hands on it."

"In the end," I echoed.

"In the end," Devon repeated. "The other private collector died about a year ago. And as part of his will, he donated the saber to a local museum, under the condition it never be sold. That amused a lot of people around here, because they knew he'd done it just to spite my father."

A hundred thousand dollars is a lot of spite. Rich people definitely lived in a different world than the one I was used to.

"Are you saying," Mike said, "that the police found this gilded saber in your dad's car?"

Devon nodded. "In the trunk."

"Did the museum people know it was missing?" I asked.

Devon nodded again. "So did most of Charleston. It was stolen a few nights ago, along with a half million dollars' worth of other antique Civil War relics."

Mike whistled.

"Well," I said. "Obviously your dad wasn't the thief. Otherwise they would have found the other stuff with the saber."

"That's just it," Devon said. "They *did* find the other missing museum stuff with the saber. All of it. In the trunk."

CHAPTER 5

"Here it is," Ralphy announced to Mike and Lisa and me. "No problem at all."

It was half an hour after Devon had told us why Mike's uncle Ted had been arrested. The police had called for Devon to go down to the station, and he'd apologized and told us he'd be back as soon as possible.

The four of us were waiting in Ralphy's guest bedroom on the third floor of Theodore Emmett's mansion. Antiques and knickknacks and oil paintings and doilies were everywhere. It was so impressive that I was sure it was the reason Ralphy had folded all his clothes and hung them neatly instead of leaving them scattered all over the floor the way he did in his own bedroom.

Mike and I moved from the windows that overlooked the park below. We crowded behind Ralphy and his laptop, peering over his shoulders to see the screen of his brand-new iBook that he loved to show off. Lisa crouched beside Ralphy.

Ralphy had pulled up the Web site of the local

newspaper and scrolled back to the news articles from a couple of days earlier. He pointed at the screen, where a photo of a sword covered half of it.

"It's all there," he said. "Do you want me to read it for you guys?"

Mike snorted. "I'm out of preschool. I know the alphabet."

"Yeah," Ralphy grinned, twisting his head to look at Mike. "But I notice your lips still move when you read, and you point to every word with your finger. When you write, do you space out every word by putting a finger down first, like kids in first grade do?"

"Hah, hah, hah," Mike said. "At least I don't keep my finger up my nose."

"How can you suggest that *I* pick my nose when *you*—"

"Gentlemen," I interrupted Ralphy as they started to get into our game of trading insults. "Speaking of nostrils, both of you need to brush your teeth or stop yakking. I can't concentrate here with your buffalo breath floating into my face."

"Hah, hah, hah," Mike and Ralphy each said. I grinned when they couldn't think of a quick insult in return, then I scanned the first few paragraphs of the article on Ralphy's computer screen.

Museum Theft Baffles Police

Charleston police were called to the Civil War museum this morning when director George Reah reported that many of the most priceless pieces were missing.

"It's unbelievable," Mr. Reah said. "While insurance will cover the value of the stolen property, many of the pieces are irreplaceable. It's as if the thief or thieves knew exactly what had the most importance in the various Civil War displays."

Although the museum is heavily monitored with electronic devices to alert authorities to any break-in attempts, a police spokesperson confirmed that no alarm occurred during the night.

"We have no indication whatsoever of how the theft occurred," the spokesperson said. "There are no signs of forced entry or other evidence to suggest the method or methods used in the robbery."

When asked if the robbery was an inside job, the spokesperson answered with a simple "no comment."

Mr. Reah believes the pieces will go to a private collector. "There is no way that the thief or thieves can pawn off the pieces or sell them at any public auction. These pieces are simply too well known, especially the gilded saber used by Sherman himself during his successful campaign through the state of Georgia."

Because of this, Mr. Reah fears the pieces may never be found. "Once they reach a private collector," he said, "they will disappear completely from public life. It is a shame that our heritage can be stolen in this manner."

Police are requesting that any members of the public with information that might help solve this crime call the police as soon as possible.

The newspaper article continued with descriptions of some of the other stolen pieces and a few comments from citizens expressing concern about the disappearance of valuable museum items. There was also a photo of the director of the museum, George Reah, facing the camera in a tweed jacket and a pipe in his mouth, like Sherlock Holmes.

"Private collector," Mike said softly.

"I know," I said with sympathy. "I was thinking the same thing. If anyone in the world is a private collector, it's your uncle."

"I can't believe he stole the stuff, though," Ralphy said. Lisa nodded her agreement.

Mike got up and began to pace around the room. His footsteps were deadened by the expensive Persian carpets.

"You don't want to believe it's him," Mike finally answered, "just because he's my uncle. I don't want to believe it's him, either."

Mike stopped pacing suddenly and craned his head to look out the window again.

"Oh, no," he groaned. "Look."

We looked.

Devon had just pulled up and parked by the sidewalk. He drove an older red Mustang.

It wasn't Devon or his car that Mike had groaned about.

It was the van that had pulled up right behind Devon's Mustang.

A van for a local television station.

We could see it clearly from our vantage point on the third floor.

As Devon began to walk toward the house, a reporter and a cameraman began to chase him up the steps.

CHAPTER 6

Earlier Devon had listened to our conversation on the front porch through the open window on the main floor.

Now was our chance to do the same. Not that we were trying to be sneaky. We just weren't sure if Devon wanted us to be out there with him as the television reporter chased him to the front door.

"How do you feel about your father being in jail right now?" the reporter asked.

She was a redhead, with an older face well baked from too much sun and too much makeup.

"Jail?" Devon said. "What makes you say he's in jail?"

"Nice try, kid," the reporter said. "A little bird told me. A little bird that wouldn't be wrong."

The redhead waved the cameraman closer. "Get him from this angle," she commanded, pointing at Devon. "The door behind him is impressive. Looks like a door belonging to a rich man."

She said in a nasty voice to Devon, "A rich man who stole from a museum."

"My father is innocent," Devon said. "Now, leave me alone."

"Tell us, then," the reporter half snarled, "did your father do it because of the financial difficulties of his real-estate venture?"

"No!" Devon sounded trapped.

"So it is true that your father is in financial trouble."

"That's not what I said!"

"Well, is it true?"

"Leave me alone," Devon answered. "Please."

"Just let me get this straight. Your father's in jail, and you deny his financial troubles."

"Quit trying to put words into my mouth." Devon clicked open the door.

"Get this shot," the redhead said to the cameraman. "The kid running from the truth."

She and the cameraman stood on the steps of the front porch.

Devon fell for her trick. Instead of continuing inside, he stopped, holding the door half open. It was a camera shot we would see on the news that night. It showed many of the expensive antiques and oil paintings.

"Leave my father and me alone," Devon said. That cry also showed on the news later, with his face distorted by anger. It made him look like a rich, spoiled young man, something I guessed the redhead wanted so the story would be more dramatic.

"Last question, then," the reporter said. "Police have suspected all along that this was an inside job. Is it just a coincidence that you work at the museum? Or did you help your father steal the half million dollars' worth of Civil War relics?"

The frozen shock on Devon's face spoke far more loudly than anything he might have answered. That, too, we saw on the news later, in the early evening.

"Go!" Devon said. "Just go!"

"I'll just camp out here all day until you have a complete conversation with me."

I was peeking through the screen of the open window, and I saw the smirk on her face.

"Leave," Devon said, with the television camera still rolling. "Or I'll call the police."

"You're sure you want the police here, too?"

I tilted my head back and began barking. Loud. Mean. Like I was a Doberman.

Mike and Ralphy and Lisa stared at me as if I had begun to roll around with rabies.

I pointed at them and motioned for them to begin barking with me. They stared at one another for a couple of seconds, then shrugged.

And barked.

And howled.

I shouted above them. "Devon, they're loose. I'm not sure I can hold them back!"

The redheaded reporter immediately backed off the porch. I grinned and pumped a fist with triumph.

That spurred Mike and Ralphy to howl and bark even louder.

The redhead and her cameraman scurried back even farther. Unfortunately, they stopped on the lawn. Far enough away that they could jump into the van and escape. But close enough to still shout questions at Devon.

"Were you working at the museum the day of the robbery?" she called toward the house.

I barely heard her above the barking.

Devon ran into the room we were in.

"Good thinking, guys," he said, his face still flushed red with anger and frustration. "Keep barking. I've got an idea."

He ran out of the room, toward the back of the house.

"And what about your previous charges?" the redhead shouted. "And the time you spent in jail?"

Devon couldn't answer because he wasn't here.

A second later I discovered the brilliant idea he'd decided to use. Because, as he told us later, he'd gone to the control panel near the garage and bumped ahead a timer switch.

Without warning, all the sprinklers on the lawn shot water in all directions.

"Aaaack!" the redhead screamed. She was wearing a long beige dress and black high heels. She jumped out of the way of one blast of water right into another. It soaked her completely.

She turned and bolted another direction, right into the cameraman. He fell backward on top of a sprinkler head. She tripped over him.

As they rolled and fought to get up, the water soaked them more.

She managed to get to her feet first.

She kicked the cameraman in the side of his lower calf and then marched to the van.

His revenge?

He filmed her as she walked away, mud and grass on her back, her hair soaked.

As she reached the sidewalk, her hair fell off her head. *A wig!*

It lay at her feet like a drowned cat.

She screamed and picked it up, then noticed the cameraman filming her.

She ran toward him, screaming, "Stop it, stop it!"

He calmly stepped aside.

The redhead slipped and fell.

He walked to the back of the van and opened the doors.

"Give me that film," she screamed. The water was still gushing all around her. "I want it now!"

The woman didn't realize she was holding her wig in her right hand. She raised a fist to shake at the cameraman, noticed her wig, screamed in rage again, and began stomping to the van.

Only the ground was wet, and as she stomped, her high heels jammed themselves into the soil.

She nearly tripped, but the straps of her shoes broke instead. She managed to keep her balance and slid and slipped toward the van in her stocking feet.

By then, of course, Mike and Ralphy and Lisa had stopped barking.

So we clearly heard the ringing of the cell phone as she opened the passenger door of the van.

Dripping with water, she reached inside and pulled it to her ear.

"What?!" she snarled.

Then her face lost all anger.

"Really?" She listened intently. "This is too good!"

She hung up the phone.

"Devon Emmett!" she yelled. "How do you feel now that your father has confessed to the crime?"

CHAPTER 7

That night I fell asleep thinking about family. I'd unpacked my suitcase earlier and found a teddy bear that my little brother, Joel, had hidden inside. He must have left it there thinking it would comfort me. Even at six years old, he adored that teddy bear. It was a big sacrifice for him to send it with me, and seeing the teddy bear gave me a touch of homesickness.

I missed Joel. I missed my mom and dad. And I missed my baby sister, Rachel, especially because she was too young to talk when I'd called home from the phone in the guest room just before crawling into bed around ten o'clock that night.

Mike's uncle Ted had not returned by the evening. Devon had not been in the mood for talking. Dinner had consisted of pizza delivered to our door by a driver who had peeked inside and asked if this was really the place where that millionaire guy lived who was now in jail, and that hadn't helped Devon's mood at all.

The news on television had been filled with the

story on Ted Emmett, and Mike had been really quiet all night. Ralphy and Lisa and I felt sorry for him because we remembered how excited Mike had been to finally visit the uncle he'd heard so much about but had never met.

So after the depressing evening of awkward conversation, the last thing I'd done before going to my room was make a collect call home.

Not that I was homesick.

Okay, a little.

Especially when Mom had put the phone up to my baby sister and let me listen to her babble for a few minutes.

Listening to her, I pictured our own home. It was a lot smaller than this giant mansion. The furniture wasn't as fancy. It didn't have a sixty-inch television and a room set aside as a small theatre like in this house. My bedroom had baseball posters instead of oil paintings like the guest room where I was staying.

But money doesn't buy love. And that's all I could think of as I listened to Rachel and remembered her blond curls and the way her face broke into a smile all the time.

She was at the age where she could almost run but still not talk. It seemed like she never walked places, but tried to zoom, as if she were so excited about being alive that she wanted to get as much out of each minute as possible.

She also had a short memory, which was great. If you left the room and returned a few minutes later, she would hurry over as fast as she could and throw her arms around your legs as if she hadn't seen you in five years.

Some people believe in God because they look around

the world and see amazing things in science or astronomy. For me, that did make it easier to understand that some great power I could never comprehend had designed our universe.

But the bigger reason I believed in God was because of love. What good would it do to live in an incredible place—no matter how amazing the design—if your soul always felt empty?

Whenever I hugged my little sister, I was able to understand better how life had more meaning because of love.

This wasn't something I talked about with Mike or Ralphy. And it was usually only something I thought about in quiet times, like now in the big dark guest room of the mansion that overlooked the park in Charleston.

Love, it seemed to me, was something invisible but stronger than anything visible in our world. And where would this love come from but from God?

Thinking about that got me to thinking about what heaven might be like. Forever, after all, was a long time. Did God expect us to spend forever flying around like angels and singing hymns of praise? To me, that would be more like eternal punishment. Especially for everyone else around who would have to listen to my voice.

Maybe heaven was a place where time didn't exist. Or where we could step outside of time. Maybe we'd be able to explore other planets or other galaxies. Maybe . . .

I fell asleep thinking of angels.

And woke thinking of angels.

Because a bright light was shining directly into my face.

"What is it?" I asked when I finally figured out Mike was shining his keychain penlight in my eyes.

"Did you know that when your eyes are closed, I can see veins in your eyelids?"

I dropped my head back on my pillow and sighed. "You woke me up to tell me that?"

"No," he answered. "Something weird is happening."

I sat up. The bedcover fell to my waist.

Mike flashed his penlight on my chest. "Is that a hair?"

I stood in my sweatpants, grabbed a T-shirt, and threw it on. "Very funny. What weird thing is happening?"

"Devon."

"Devon?"

"I couldn't fall asleep. I was lying in my bed and I heard him walk down the hallway, so I decided to get up and ask him some questions. Except I saw him tiptoe out the back door."

"Mike, what time is it?"

"Just after midnight."

"You woke me up just after midnight to tell me about someone walking around his own house?"

"Thing is, when I got to the back door, it seemed like he was talking with someone in—"

A bright light suddenly flared in the darkness beyond my bedroom window. Mike darted to the window. In my sweats and a T-shirt, I joined him.

We stared below at the courtyard. Specifically, at the garage in the rear of the courtyard.

Where curtains of flames rose along the exterior walls.

CHAPTER 8

"Ralphy!" Mike shouted as we ran through the mansion. "Ralphy! Wake up! Call the fire department!"

Running behind Mike, I called out, "Why don't I do it?"

"No," he shouted without slowing down. "You have to help me."

I stayed close. "Help you?"

"Devon!" he said. "I think Devon is in the garage!"

"What?!"

Mike didn't answer, just kept running. He skidded through a turn on the hardwood floors, dashed through the kitchen at the back of the house, and pounded open the back door.

We rushed through the courtyard, down the narrow cobblestone walks that led past all the vines and bushes.

The flames on the outside of the wall were as high as the garage roof. A low roar seemed to fill the air.

"There!" Mike pointed.

The side door to the garage was open. The light of the flames clearly showed that a pair of legs stuck out. Horizontally. Toes up. Which meant that Devon was on the concrete floor, with the rest of his upper body inside.

Mike pointed. "We have to pull him out!"

I barely heard his voice above the roaring of the flames. So instead of yelling back, I nodded and stepped forward with Mike. I raised my arm to shield my face from the heat.

The intensity of the growing fire drove us to our knees. Lower to the ground, the air was cooler. That was Devon's only hope for survival.

We crawled toward him.

Without warning, a deluge of water hit us on our backs. I didn't look behind me to see where it came from, but the cold blast made it easier to reach Devon.

I grabbed one foot. Mike grabbed the other.

"Ready?" I shouted.

"Ready!"

With the water still spraying us, we straightened and pulled.

Devon's body slid toward us.

More water gushed into our faces and chests as we strained to pull Devon away from the garage and toward the mansion.

One step.

Two steps.

Finally we were clear of the heat and the flames.

And the water stopped.

I looked toward the mansion.

Lisa stood there with the garden hose in her hands, grinning.

"Thanks," I said. "Couldn't have done it without you."

"No time," Mike said. "No time."

"What?" We were clear. Devon was already struggling to sit up, shaking the water off his face.

"No time." Mike tried to pull Devon to his feet. "Come on, we've got to move."

"Mike . . ."

"The Mercedes," he said.

"The Mercedes? It's too late to do anything about the car. We don't have a hope of going in there and—"

I stopped.

The Mercedes!

"Devon, get moving." Mike was lifting him under one arm. I lifted under the other. Lisa helped us support him as we staggered toward the back of the mansion.

Ralphy had wandered outside to see what we were doing. "Called the fire department," he said.

"Get inside, Ralphy!" Mike said. "Now!"

"Huh?"

"The Mercedes!"

Ralphy didn't understand. We pushed him through the open back door of the mansion. Mike slammed the door shut.

"The Mercedes," he repeated.

I nodded, sucking in air. It felt like the inside of my throat was sandpaper. The smell of smoke filled my nostrils.

"The Mercedes," I said. "The gas tank. It's going to—"

I didn't have a chance to finish.

The explosion from inside the garage mushroomed outward with a thunderous bang. Most of the kitchen windows shattered from the blast. A heartbeat later, shards of wood and brick rained against the back side of the mansion.

I slumped against the wall and sat as sirens reached us from the distance.

Devon lowered himself and sat beside me. He stared straight ahead and said nothing. He threw something in the air with his right hand and caught it. When he tossed it up again, he missed it and it bounced on the floor.

A cuff link.

I glanced at it and gave it back to him. He tossed it again and again and said nothing. His depression was like a black cloud of smoke that had followed him in from the garage fire.

"Come on," Mike said to try to cheer him up. "At least it can't get any worse."

"Don't bet on it," Devon said dully. He tossed the cuff link in the air again. A second explosion reached us, this one smaller than the first. And seconds later, half a lawnmower blade smashed through one of the remaining kitchen windows and clattered onto the floor.

Devon forced a grin across his face. "See?"

Mike looked at Devon. "But your father has a great insurance policy, right?"

Devon gave us a look that was difficult to understand. Then he said something even more difficult to figure out. "A lot of good insurance does a person who's going to die."

CHAPTER 9

By one in the morning, the fire was out. The massive fire trucks had departed, the firemen in their uniforms no longer dashing in all directions in the night. The neighbors had stopped gawking and had returned to their homes.

Beyond the courtyard, all that remained of the garage were large pieces of water-soaked charcoal where the roof had collapsed in the middle of walls burnt almost to the foundation. With the wreckage of an exploded Mercedes beneath all the charred wood.

We weren't about to sleep, however.

The police were still at the mansion.

Talking to Devon in the dining room. With me and Mike and Ralphy sitting quietly on chairs at the table.

We hadn't had a chance to shower or change clothes, so the room smelled of soot.

"One more time," the smaller of the two officers said to Devon. His uniform was neatly pressed, and he had a huge mustache. The other officer was large in a rumpled uniform, and he kept yawning. "You heard a noise, you walked to the garage, stepped inside, and someone hit you on the back of the head. That's it. No chance of identifying who did it."

"No chance," Devon said. His eyes shifted sideways. He took a breath and then looked the smaller officer square in the eyes. "No chance at all."

"Any guesses?" The smaller officer consulted his notepad. "After all, the firemen tell me that all signs point to arson. They say a preliminary guess is that gasoline was soaked all around the outside walls."

"Guesses?" Devon repeated.

"Yeah. Like does anyone hate you or your father? Anyone want to get him back for anything?"

"Not that I can think of."

"Could it be someone burned—pardon the pun—in your father's real-estate venture?" This came from the larger officer, who spoke as if he really were half asleep.

"I don't know what you mean," Devon said. He squirmed in his chair.

The larger officer suddenly leaned forward. His voice lost all sleepiness as his eyes widened and he stared at Devon. "Spare me the lies, kid. It's all over town that your father needs money badly to keep the real-estate deal from collapsing. You know it, too. Which makes me wonder what else you're hiding from us. I don't buy the fact that you just wandered into the garage and got hit. If you want us to believe you got hit on the back of the head without seeing who did it, why is there a large bruise across your nose and eye?"

"It's where I landed. If you check the back of my head, you'll find a bigger bruise." As if confirming that, Devon reached up and touched the back of his skull and winced at the pain.

"What about the smell of gasoline? Didn't that make you a little worried?"

Devon didn't reply.

The officer leaned in closer. "That's right. Gasoline. If the firemen have it right, the walls were soaked with the stuff. You should have been able to smell it halfway there from the house. But you still went inside?"

Devon spoke quietly. "I heard a noise."

"Or maybe there was no intruder," the larger officer said. "Maybe you're the one who started the fire. Maybe you're looking for insurance money for the building and the vehicle to help pay your father's legal fees."

"I'm tired," Devon said. "I want to go to sleep."

"That's all you have to say?"

"I walked in. Someone hit me in the head. Now I'm tired and I want to go to sleep."

"Fine." Both officers stood as the larger one kept speaking. "But don't expect this to be the last of it."

Mike wandered into my bedroom half an hour later. I'd been able to shower and change into another pair of sweats and T-shirt. The clothes I'd worn earlier, like Mike's and

Devon's clothing, were in a large plastic garbage bag because they were so smoky and singed with holes from sparks that we had no choice but to throw them out.

I was sitting on the edge of my bed, staring toward the window.

"Ralphy's asleep now," Mike said. "Lisa's in her room. I wanted to talk to you about this without anyone else knowing."

"About Devon, right?"

"He lied," Mike said. "To the police."

"I know."

"You do?"

"Yeah. Why didn't you say anything to the police, then?"

"His word against mine," Mike answered. "Plus, he must have had a good reason for lying. I mean, I know he didn't start the fire himself."

Mike paused. "Why didn't you tell the police?"

"Same reason."

Mike moved to the window and looked down on where the garage had been. "How did you know he was lying?"

"His toes were pointing up," I said. "If someone had hit him on the back of the head, he would have fallen face forward. He wouldn't have landed on his back. How did you know?"

Mike faced me again. "The reason I came here to wake you up. Remember I said I heard Devon walking down the hallway and I was going to talk with him?"

I nodded.

"He got to the back door and kept walking. I was

standing in the doorway and I watched him walk to the garage. I could see a glow of light through one of the garage windows. That's probably why he was going there. To check out the light."

"The light was on in the garage? Then he would have seen who was in there."

Mike shook his head. "I didn't say a light was on. I said there was a glow of light. Like from a flashlight. But it wasn't."

"Make sense, will you?"

"As Devon opened the side door to the garage, the glow of light quit, and I heard a slamming sound."

"Slamming?"

"My guess is the trunk lid of the Mercedes. When it was open, the trunk light was on. That caused the glow. When Devon opened the door, whoever was looking inside the trunk shut it hard. Which, of course, was the slam. After that, I heard a low voice. It sounded like the person was warning Devon to leave. That's when I ran up to your room to get your help."

I thought about it for a second. "And while you were up here, that person must have attacked Devon."

I snapped my fingers. "No. Tried to run past him. They would have wrestled in the doorway. The intruder must have won the fight, maybe punched him in the face where it's bruised. The bump on the back of Devon's head is where he landed."

"Yup," Mike said. "Just the opposite of what he told the police. But why would he lie?"

"You're right," I said. "That's the big question."

I thought of the cuff link. I had noticed the initials T.S. on it, but the letters had not clicked until now. *T.S.*

I mentioned it to Mike. "Thomas Stang?" I guessed.

"Just another question," Mike said. "Along with why Devon would lie. One more question mixed in with a bunch of others just as big."

CHAPTER 10

We were supposed to be here on vacation. I decided to go for a walk and see Charleston that way, not through a window of a taxi or a car.

As I moved down a quiet street, away from the river, I let my mind wander, remembering what I'd read about Charleston before getting here.

The narrow cobblestone streets and the ancient buildings pushed together made it seem like an old city in Europe. Because there were no people around me, it was easy to imagine that I was over a hundred years back in time. I thought of pirates and of the sadness of the slaves as they arrived here, with slave traders selling them like horses nearby at the ancient wharves.

It made me shiver, even with the quiet of the early morning streets around me.

Then I looked up and saw St. Michael's steeple rising above the buildings around it. And I remembered what I'd read about it.

Before the Civil War, the steeple had been painted white, like a sleek angel, wings folded, rising above the city. But during the war, the whiteness of the steeple on moonlit nights had provided an easy aiming point for Yankee soldiers. At night, then, they had used it as a target for their cannons.

I imagined the high whistle of the cannonballs as they dropped from the sky, ripped through the roofs of houses, scattered the flames of fireplaces. I imagined the wails of frightened babies filling the night, imagined boys like me awake in their beds, staring at the ceiling, listening to the screaming whistle of the next cannonball, wondering if this was the cannonball that would snuff out their life when it landed. And all because of the great white steeple rising into the darkness.

I shivered again, even though it was warm.

The steeple was white now, too. But for the rest of the war, the citizens of Charleston had been forced to paint the steeple black to make it invisible in the night.

As I stepped from shadows into the early morning sunshine, the warmth on my face reminded me that I was not back in the Civil War, part of a city under siege.

I shook off the sad and terrible feelings and kept walking forward, whistling like a cheerful tourist.

I enjoyed the rest of my sightseeing, but if I had known what would later happen to me in St. Michael's steeple, I would have tried catching the next flight out of Charleston.

CHAPTER 11

"Ralphy, did you put glue in those eggs?"

The question came from Mike, who leaned over Ralphy's shoulder. Ralphy stood at the stove, stirring eggs in a frying pan to scramble them.

"No, Michael," Ralphy said, vexed at Mike's suspicion. "That is cream. Just enough to keep the eggs moist."

"What about the red stuff?"

"Curry. You'll appreciate the flavor and—"

Ralphy slapped Mike's hand as Mike tried to scoop some out with his fingers. "Not till it's ready."

Mike licked the moist egg off his index finger. "Not bad."

I was kneeling on the kitchen counter, taping a piece of cardboard across one of the broken windows. Most of the kitchen windows were covered. I'd been busy for half an hour already.

"Come on," I groaned to Mike. "I have to eat from that. Like I want your dirty fingerprints in my eggs."

It was eight in the morning and there was no wind and no cloud cover. A beautiful stillness hung over the courtyard. But the tranquility was ruined by the wisps of smoke still coming up from the burned-down garage.

I wondered why Devon hadn't come down yet from his bedroom. Mike had already swept the kitchen floor clean of broken glass. Ralphy had been clattering with pots and pans as he began breakfast. Lisa was upstairs getting ready for the day.

"You watch the cooking channel, Ralphy?" Mike asked.

"I'm not telling."

"Hah! That means you do."

"I'm a well-rounded individual," Ralphy said, lowering a cover on the frying pan. "Which means your scrambled eggs will be perfect. Any complaints?"

"None," Mike said happily. "I could be a bachelor forever. Hang out with you guys. Eat your food. Only problem is I'll need someone to do my laundry. Think Devon will help?"

"If he ever gets out of bed," I answered. I taped the last corner of the cardboard in place, then saw movement in the courtyard through one of the windows that wasn't broken. "Correction. Looks like Devon has been up for a while."

Devon probably didn't see me on the counter inside the mansion, because he stopped at a small birdbath in the middle of the courtyard. He tilted it, spilling water out of the top. With his back toward me, he squatted, as if he were placing something beneath the base of the birdbath. Then he stood and walked to the back door.

He stepped inside and drew a deep breath.

"Smells like breakfast," he said. "What a great idea."

But he didn't get a chance to eat.

Three minutes later the police showed up again. To do the same thing they'd done to his father about twenty-four hours earlier. With them was Thomas Stang, the skinny middle-aged man who was Theodore Emmett's business partner.

And the first thing Stang did was grab Devon by the collar of his shirt and threaten to kill him.

CHAPTER 12

"Where is it?" Stang demanded as he pulled Devon up from his chair in the dining room. Devon's napkin fell to the floor, and his hand shot outward, knocking his plate off the table.

"Tell me, you hoodlum. Now. Before I strangle you bare-handed."

I was surprised at Stang's strength. And at his temper. He wore a dark blue business suit and, with his wispy graying hair, seemed much more like an accountant than the savage caveman that he was imitating.

"Sir!" This was from the smaller of the two police officers. It was the same pair that had grilled Devon after the firemen left, only hours earlier. "We're here to handle this. Sir!"

Stang didn't let go. The heels of his flat dress shoes squashed the eggs and toast that had fallen onto the floor from Devon's plate. He shook Devon like a terrier trying to snap a rat's neck. "I want the disk!"

Surprised as I was that Stang was so strong

and so violent, I was more surprised that Devon didn't fight back. Devon was taller and bigger and younger. But he simply flopped back and forth each time that Stang shook him, not lifting his arms to protect himself.

"Sir!" Again the smaller officer tried uselessly to control Stang. "We promise you that we will arrest him!"

Stang didn't let go.

It took the larger officer to quiet things down. He reached over and slapped a hand on Stang's shoulder. He squeezed hard. His massive fingers must have found a nerve, because Stang yelped. The larger officer calmly kept his grip until Stang finally released Devon's shirt collar.

Stang rubbed his sore shoulder and glared at the big officer. The officer smiled a sleepy smile. I was beginning to understand his sleepy look meant just the opposite.

"Tell him, then," Stang said, glaring. "That I want the disk. You both saw him on the surveillance tape. He downloaded something from my computer and stole it on a disk."

"He wants his disk," the big officer said. "And don't try to deny you took it."

Devon shrugged. "Since when did you guys set up video cameras in your office?"

"None of your business," Stang snarled. "But it served its purpose, didn't it? Thought you could just waltz in and steal information from my computer, didn't you?"

Devon's answer was very simple. He reached inside his shirt and pulled out a floppy disk. He threw it at Stang.

"Satisfied?"

"Not until you're arrested," Stang answered.

Stang motioned the police forward.

They cuffed Devon and led him out of the mansion.

CHAPTER 13

"Now what?"

I arrived on the front porch just as Ralphy asked Mike that question.

"What do you mean, now what?"

I sat beside them. They were in rocking chairs, and I leaned back in mine. Lisa was with us, too, gently rocking in her chair. It was a wonderful, relaxing moment in a summer in the south. Except for all the stuff that had happened in the last twenty-four hours. Ted Emmett's arrest. An arson fire. And now Devon's arrest.

"Well, your uncle Ted is in jail," Ralphy continued. "From what I understand, since he confessed, he won't be released on bail. Devon is gone now, too. Now what? Fly home?"

"Drink lemonade," Mike answered. He took a sip from his glass. It was beaded with water that had condensed on the sides. In front of us, tourists walked quietly, gawking at the mansion. Mike waved lazily, like he owned the place.

"Drink lemonade?" Ralphy couldn't relax. But

then, he never did. "But, but . . ."

"Ralphy," Mike said. "It will cost too much money to change our tickets to fly back early. What else can we do except guard Uncle Ted's house?"

Mike looked at his watch. "It's only nine o'clock. Later this morning we'll take a taxi and go visit Uncle Ted. We'll also meet with his attorney, who will give us advice on what to do next."

Mike took another sip of lemonade and waved lazily.

"I'm impressed," Ralphy said. "You're so calm about all of this."

"That's the kind of guy I am," Mike answered, buffing his nails against his shirt.

Lisa finally spoke. "Yup," she said. "The kind of guy who called home to ask his mother if we should fly home early. The kind of guy who listened very carefully when she told him to visit his uncle Ted and then ask the attorney any other questions."

"Oh," Ralphy said, punching Mike's shoulder. "That kind of guy."

Mike shrugged.

"Speaking of money to change the flight home," Ralphy said, "what I can't figure out is why your uncle spent the money on our tickets in the first place. I mean, all we've been hearing is how his real-estate deal is putting him in so much financial trouble."

"Good question."

"I've got another one," I said. "Who tipped off the police to look in the trunk of the Mercedes for the saber and the other stuff stolen from the museum?"

"Easy," Mike grunted. "Same person who stole it and put it in his trunk."

"Mike?" Ralphy shook his head at Mike's slowness. "Mike, your uncle confessed. Why confess if he didn't do it?"

"Which brings us back in a circle," I added. "If your uncle didn't do it, why confess? But if he did do it, who knew it was in the trunk of his car?"

"And who knew the Mercedes was here?" Lisa asked. "Your uncle Ted was at a golf tournament. A person would think, then, that the Mercedes should have been at the country club."

I thought of Tom Stang picking us up the morning of the tournament in his black Navigator. I thought of the cuff link with the initials T.S. I thought of Devon breaking into Stang's office. I wondered if it would be stupid to mention all of this. But Mike spoke before I could decide.

"Uncle Ted didn't do it." Mike was no longer sitting back in his rocker as if he were the rich owner of the mansion.

"You want to believe that because he's your uncle."

"No, I'm saying that because anyone smart enough to make the money it took to buy this house is not careless enough to leave stolen museum pieces in his trunk."

"Good point," Ralphy said.

Mike looked sheepish. "Actually, Mom pointed that out to me during our phone call."

"Let's go with that," I said. "Your uncle is innocent."

"And . . ."

"And we do something about it," I answered Mike. "If we don't, who else will?"

"All right, Sherlock," he said, "where do you suggest we start?"

I smiled. I told them my thoughts about Tom Stang.

And I showed them why I'd taken a few minutes to join them on the front porch.

It was the computer disk I'd found under the base of the birdbath in the courtyard.

CHAPTER 14

Lisa and I leaned over Ralphy's shoulder. We stared at the computer screen of his laptop. Mike was pacing the room behind us.

Ralphy's fingers clicked rapidly. Seconds later numbers and names filled the screen.

"This is weird," Ralphy said. "Very weird."

Mike marched over and surveyed the screen.

"Now I'm impressed," Mike said. "It took you less than a second to read all that and come up with your conclusion."

"I've already seen this."

"What?" I spoke as I squinted to read the screen better.

"About an hour ago. Just before breakfast. It came to me by e-mail."

"Let me get this straight," Mike said. "Same file?"

"Same file."

"I think these are accounts," I told them. "Look. Numbers. Then names of people. Then . . ."

I figured out what I was reading. "Names of

stocks. If this disk came from the Stang and Emmett Stockbrokers' office, that would make sense."

Mike snapped his fingers. "So Devon gave them a disk, knowing he had a backup anyway."

"Must be it," I said.

"Hang on, guys." Ralphy clicked his fingers across the keyboard again. "Let me pull up that e-mail."

He pointed at the screen. "There's the address it came from."

It was obvious on the screen: ts@sestockbrokers.com.

"Tom Stang at Stang and Emmett Stockbrokers.com," I said. "For some reason, Stang is appearing in all of this again."

"Why would Stang e-mail Ralphy the same information that Devon put on a . . ." Mike stopped himself. Smacked himself on the forehead. "Ralphy, let me guess. First chance you had, you showed off your computer to Devon, right?"

"It is a smoking laptop," he said. "We're talking gigabytes and gigahertz."

"I'll hertz you if you don't lay off the computer talk. Did you show it to Devon?"

"He was interested," Ralphy said defensively.

"Or he was just being polite," I said. "And did you trade e-mail addresses with him?"

"I told him I'd send some JPEGs of our trip."

"In other words," Mike said, "Devon knew about Ralphy's laptop, and Devon has his e-mail address. Right, Ralphy?"

Ralphy nodded.

Lisa spoke. "So not only did Devon back up this information on a second disk in case he lost the first, he made an extra backup by sending a copy to Ralphy."

"Which still doesn't explain why Devon broke into Stang's office." I tapped my teeth as I thought about it. "Obviously the information is important. But why?"

"If we know why the information is so valuable," Mike said, "we'll probably know why he broke in to get it."

"Thanks," I said. "That helps."

Mike smiled. Perhaps I needed to explain to him the concept of sarcasm.

"Client list?" Ralphy asked, pointing at the names. "I mean, it did come from a stockbroker's office. Maybe each account number belongs to a client, and those are the stocks they own."

"Phone book," Mike said. "Let's look up some of these names in the local phone book. If we find them there, chances are they will be clients."

"Wow," I said. "And you didn't even call your mom about that."

Mike grinned. Then his grin froze in place.

"You hear that?" he said.

Ralphy and Lisa nodded.

I nodded.

Downstairs, a noise came from the kitchen.

CHAPTER 15

A minute later the three of us reached Theodore Emmett's Civil War room. We'd asked Lisa to stay upstairs and call the police if we didn't return in five minutes.

"You were right," Mike whispered to me, gesturing at all the Civil War pieces around us. "No better place."

I put a finger to my lips, then pointed Mike at a nearby mannequin of a soldier in a Confederate uniform. I made a slicing motion.

He understood.

He reached for the sword in the sheath attached to the mannequin's waist and began to pull.

He frowned.

Pulled harder.

And the mannequin began to topple!

I darted beneath it and held it up.

Mike grinned.

He pulled again and the sword came loose. I set the soldier upright.

Ralphy had already taken a sword from the

second dressed-up soldier.

That left none for me.

I looked around desperately. Saw an old musket pistol in an unlocked display case.

I tiptoed over and grabbed it.

Mike looked at me as if I were crazy.

I shrugged.

Noises were coming from the kitchen. *What if it's the person who planted the stolen stuff in Ted Emmett's Mercedes?*

"Ready?" I whispered.

Both of them nodded.

We crept forward.

Down the hallway where ancient oil portraits stared down on us.

Past the dining room with the huge table where only the night before the two cops had grilled Devon with questions.

Past a room with a huge fireplace.

And on to the kitchen.

"On three," I whispered. "Got it? One, two, three, and we jump on the guy."

Again both of them nodded. Ralphy's messy, straight-up hair and his wide-eyed, frightened expression was a contrast to Mike's mean, almost angry concentration.

They raised their swords high.

I lifted my pistol musket.

"One . . ." I whispered.

"Two . . ."

Before I could say "three," Ralphy screamed a war whoop and charged forward.

"Three . . ." I finished weakly and Mike and I followed him into the kitchen.

And there she was.

A tall brunette. In a blue jean skirt. Wearing a man's white button-up shirt over a blue T-shirt.

"Caught me red-handed," she said, holding her hands high. "Please, don't hurt me."

CHAPTER 16

She smiled, then put her hands back down.

"Let me guess," she said, still smiling. "You must be Mike, Devon's cousin. And the rest of you are his friends."

Without waiting for an answer, she turned her back on us and lifted something from the counter. She faced us again and waved a slice of toast. "Devon's shown me photos of you, of course. Hard not to recognize that red hair."

She took a bite and waited for us to say something.

None of us did. We were too startled by her appearance. By her confidence. And by her lack of fear.

"So what's with the Civil War attack?" she said after swallowing her first bite. "Did Devon put you up to this? Did he want to see if you could make me scream?"

She looked past us.

"Nice try, Devon," she called. "I suppose you were hoping to get this on video or something."

"Um . . ." I said.

She smiled. "Yes?"

"Who are you?" I asked.

"A thief who wanted to break in to get something to eat." She rolled her eyeballs. "Samantha Evans. Devon's girlfriend. He didn't tell you about me?"

"It's been a little crazy since yesterday morning," Mike explained.

"I can imagine. I heard about your reputation from Devon. Were you the one who broke the kitchen windows?"

The pieces of cardboard were taped in place, hiding most of the courtyard from our view.

"Actually," I said, "the craziness is about Devon. And his father. They've both been arrested."

Samantha laughed. "Right."

She called over my shoulder. "Devon! Nice try! It's not April Fool's Day."

"Really," she said, "what's been happening?"

"You came in the front, didn't you?" I answered.

She took another bite of toast and nodded. "I've got my own key."

"Went straight to the cupboard and fridge?" I continued.

She nodded as she chewed.

"Didn't really look out that one last little piece of window that's not taped down by cardboard, right?"

She swallowed and nodded.

"Take a close look at the garage," I said.

She turned around and leaned on the counter as she

stood on her tiptoes for a view.

When she turned back to us, her face had lost all of its casual amusement.

"A fire?"

"Last night," Mike said. "Uncle Ted was arrested before. Devon after."

She wanted to talk outside, but away from the view of anyone walking down the street. So we called for Lisa and joined Samantha in the courtyard, a short walk out the back door from the kitchen area.

The scent of flowers was mixed with the smoky smell of the burned wood of the garage. The sun was already very hot, and the drone of insects filled the background.

"Arrested," she repeated.

"Haven't you been watching the news?" Mike asked.

She shook her head. "I'm taking a summer session university course, and I've spent the last day locked in my room, working on a term paper. Which was why I was looking forward to seeing Devon today. The last time I saw him was the night before last. The night you guys came in. I remember, because Devon was telling me all about you while we drove to Savannah. We were going to borrow his dad's Mercedes, but my Mustang was back from repairs, so we went in that instead."

"That's your Mustang that Devon was driving yesterday?" Mike asked. "Cool car."

"Fun to drive, too. There was an arts festival in Savannah I wanted to see. We had a great time. And now you tell me both of them are in jail?"

Mike explained. So far, Ralphy hadn't said a word. Just kept staring at her and then blushing and looking away when she glanced at him. I didn't blame him. She was Devon's age and cute enough that I understood why Ralphy was tongue-tied.

"I find this so difficult to believe." Samantha had a deep southern accent. "Ted, stealing from the museum?"

"Does that mean you'd find it easy to believe Devon broke into Stang's office?" I asked, hoping she wouldn't get mad at me.

Samantha smiled ruefully. "He's had a rough past. Drugs and petty theft. I thought, though, since he and his dad started going to the church that I attend that things had changed. I mean, it's been a year since Devon was in any kind of trouble. He got that great job at the museum and really turned his life around."

She stared off into the distance. "No, I still refuse to think that Devon had me fooled. If he broke into the office there was a good reason. And his dad? Why would he have set up a trust fund to donate a million dollars to the church's charities if he was going to steal—"

She stopped herself. Sighed.

"I wish sometimes I could hit a rewind button and take back some of the words that come out of my mouth. Will you pretend I didn't say anything about the trust fund?

Devon would be furious at me if he knew I'd let that slip out."

We nodded. But it was in the back of my mind. The same question that Samantha had begun to ask. If Ted Emmett was in such financial trouble, why had he been arranging to donate money to a trust fund? Why had he paid for our flights here to Charleston?

Samantha jolted me out of my thoughts by snapping her fingers.

"Hey," she said. "Did you tell me that the police had found the stolen museum pieces in the white Mercedes?"

"Yup." This came from Mike.

"Ted hasn't been driving it," Samantha said. "Devon has. Devon's own car is getting repaired. For the last week, he's been borrowing the Mercedes and Ted has been walking to work. If Ted stole the pieces, why would he have left them in the car that Devon was driving?"

She stood up.

"Does this mean that Devon really is the thief?" she asked.

She began to cry.

CHAPTER 17

In a doorway at the corner of King Street and Broad, Mike suddenly reached out as if he were catching a fly from the air. He moved his closed fist toward his mouth and pretended to eat the fly.

"Healthy," Lisa said sarcastically. "You should consider becoming a vegetarian."

"No thanks," Mike said. "Think of all the things that could wrong."

Lisa gave him a puzzled look.

"Dogs could bite you," he explained. "Horses could kick you. Animals are too dangerous. Then to try to work on them when they're injured or sick? No thanks."

"Vegetarian, Mike," Lisa said. "Not veterinarian."

"Whatever." He grinned. "Come on. I knew the difference. Really."

Veterinarian. Vegetarian. I could tell he was bored if he was making those kinds of pathetic jokes.

"Hang in there, Mike," I said. "Let's give this

another half hour."

Back at the Emmett mansion, Ralphy was working on the phone book to match names to accounts in the file from Thomas Stang. Here, we had already been waiting for an hour, watching the entrance to an old, stone-walled two-story building across the street. The other buildings up and down the street were just as ancient. Art stores. Old restaurants. Real-estate offices. And every ten minutes or so, another horse-drawn carriage went by, with the guy at the reins telling the tourists stories about old Charleston.

"Half hour?" he answered. "Lisa, if you want to tell Ricky this is a silly idea, I'll agree with you."

"Come on," I said before Lisa could agree. "What else can we do?"

"Let's see," Mike said. "We're in a city we've never visited before. It has a giant aquarium. Horse-drawn carriage rides. Places to go fishing. Beaches about twenty minutes away. I don't know, pal. What else can we do besides stand in this doorway and wait for a stockbroker so we can follow him around town?"

"Let your uncle get blamed for a crime he didn't do?"

"You had to bring that up. Just when I had totally been able to get that out of my mind."

"Right," I said, knowing that was all he could think of.

I knew Mike's irritation level was rising for two reasons. He couldn't get his uncle's troubles out of his mind. And he hated doing nothing. Even if he had agreed it was one of the only options.

"Let me go through this again, Mike. No one is telling us anything about the situation. Not your uncle Ted. He's still in jail and our meeting with him isn't until later today. His lawyer can't tell us anything because of the simple fact we still haven't met his lawyer and, oh yes, his lawyer is busy with all the charges against both your uncle and cousin. Devon's girlfriend can't tell us. She ran away without explaining why. And we don't want to call your mother again because it will get her even more worried and we don't have anything to tell her."

Mike let out a deep breath. "But this waiting and waiting is—"

"I know. Killing you. But Devon must have had a good reason for breaking into Stang's office and getting that list. And Stang was pretty upset when he asked for the disk. That list must mean something. Stang's got something to do with all of this."

"It wouldn't be so bad if I thought waiting here would lead to something. But we don't even know if Stang has a back entrance. For all we know, he's already left somewhere in his car. And even if he does walk out the front, how do we know that's actually going to help?"

"We agreed to take the chance that this might not help," Lisa pointed out. "Remember?"

"How about I just go up there and see if he's still in his office?" Mike said. "I hate doing nothing."

My turn to let out a deep breath. "If he's up to something, the last thing we want to do is let him know we're interested in him. Remember, your uncle Ted told us that every day they both walk to a restaurant for lunch. And it's nearly noon. So maybe . . ."

It was a silly idea. I quit talking and sat down and

rested my head against my knees. I should have stayed back with Ralphy and tried to help him as he surfed the Net to find out more about the stock market.

"Guys!" Lisa said.

I looked up. She was pointing across the street at the entrance to the office. At a tall man in a tweed jacket, who bit on a Sherlock Holmes type of pipe, even though it wasn't lit. He'd entered the building about five minutes earlier.

"We've just learned something very interesting," she said.

"That I'm now very confused?" Mike said.

"Knew it all along," Lisa told him. "But there's something else. That man with the pipe in his mouth?"

Mike and I nodded.

"When he went in, he seemed familiar," she continued. "And I've just figured out where I've seen him before. From the newspaper article that Ralphy pulled up on the Internet. He's George Reah. Director of the Civil War museum."

"And this might mean . . ."

"Mike," I said, understanding why Lisa thought this was significant. "The police believe the theft was an inside job. Devon works at the museum. They believe Devon helped your uncle steal the pieces. But if Devon and your uncle are innocent, and if Stang has something to do with all of this—"

"—now we have a connection between Stang and someone inside the museum," Lisa finished for me.

"Just more questions, though," Mike said.

"I know," I agreed with him. "And I've been thinking about this while we've been waiting. I believe we can call someone who could give us a lot of answers."

CHAPTER 18

The entrance to the South Carolina Aquarium overlooked the harbor. Inside, I knew from the brochure, were sharks in a huge aquarium, along with all sorts of other incredible sea life. Maybe an octopus. Lobsters. Cool stuff.

But Mike and I weren't here to go inside.

Instead, we waited near the entrance. To our right was a long wooden staircase that led down to the river's edge, where a steamboat waited to take tourists to Sumter Island.

"See it?" I said to Mike, pointing at a smudge low on the river.

"Huh? The seagull that looks like it's ready to dive-bomb an innocent tourist?"

"No. Not the seagull. That island smack-dab in the middle of the water. The Ashley and Cooper Rivers meet just before it, then flow together out to the Atlantic. That island was in a perfect position to guard the river during the Civil War. See, without it, cannonballs fired from one shore would not have been able to reach the other shore and vice versa. But with the island, cannons could fire in either direction and reach both shores. That meant no ship could pass by on either side unless the soldiers on the island let them."

"Good," Mike said. I doubted he'd pass the test if I asked him what I'd just told him. "Where's the redhead?"

"And Fort Sumter is also famous because it's where the first shot was fired to start the Civil War."

"You know I hate waiting," he said. "She's going to come here, right?"

"But they didn't use cannonballs," I continued. "Instead, they cut up pieces of elephants and shoved them down the cannons."

"You really think this is going to work, huh." Mike looked in all directions, squinting against the sun.

"And what was really cool," I said, "was that the heat of the exploding gunpowder actually cooked the pieces of elephant. So that when the chunks landed here in Charleston, they were hard enough to do some major damage."

Mike looked at his watch. "And how do you know we can trust her?"

"But that wasn't such a bad thing. At least for the people in Charleston who didn't get hit by pieces of cooked elephant. Because the survivors had something to eat. Many of them actually began to hope the soldiers would fire potatoes at them, too, because after a while they would get tired of just having meat."

Mike tapped one of his feet against the wood beneath us. He leaned against the railing, letting the slight breeze ruffle his hair. "Think of it. What Ralphy found out about

Tom Stang was amazing. Maybe we should just take it to the police instead."

Mike hadn't heard a single thing I'd told him about the elephants. So I gave up and answered his comment.

"The police believe they have a guilty man. Ted Emmett has confessed. From their point of view, what more do they need?"

"I know, I know," Mike said. "It's just that you saw how that woman was."

"See," I corrected.

"Huh?"

"She's behind you, coming our way."

Mike turned.

It was the redheaded reporter who had earlier chased Devon Emmett into the mansion. Who had run away at the sound of us barking. And had slipped and fallen on the wet grass.

Of course, we weren't going to let her know that we had seen all of that.

We waved. We knew who she was, but she didn't know us. Except through the telephone conversation through which I'd arranged this meeting.

"Hello," we both said when she reached us.

"You guys wanted this meeting?" she said, impatience in her voice. "You're just kids."

"Doesn't mean what we know can't help you." Mike grinned. "You do want a great news story about my uncle Ted Emmett, don't you?"

"Your uncle?" she said, suddenly interested.

Mike nodded.

"Let me repeat, nephew or not, you're just kids. You promised me something good over the telephone. I don't want to find out I'm wasting my time."

"We'll give you as much information as we can," Mike said. "But we want to trade for whatever information you can give us."

"Give me one good reason why," she demanded.

"Because if my uncle is innocent, won't that make a great news story? And won't it be good for you if you're the one to break it?"

"Maybe . . ." She frowned. "But how do I know you have any information to trade?"

"Remember when you were in the van outside the Emmett mansion and you got the call that said Ted Emmett had just confessed?" I asked.

She nodded. I didn't think it was a good time to mention her wig and how it had fallen off just before the call.

"I'll bet I can tell you who it was," I continued.

"What makes you think I even know?"

"Caller ID on your cell phone. Or some other way. I don't think a news journalist as good as you would be satisfied until you did find out."

"All right, then, so I know. What about it?"

"If I guess right, will you take us seriously?"

She smiled.

"One guess," I said. "Thomas Stang."

She tapped a fingernail against her front tooth.

"Let me buy you guys burgers and shakes," she said. "Let's talk."

"Sure," Mike said. "Lunch was at least a half hour ago."

As we walked away, Mike said to her, "Isn't that cool about the history of how the Yankee soldiers fed the people of Charleston?"

"Huh?"

"How they fired pieces of elephants at the——"

Mike gasped as I elbowed him.

"Could we start," I said to the reporter, "with what you know about the real-estate deal that is about to bankrupt Ted Emmett's corporation?"

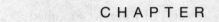

CHAPTER 19

"This is what I know right now," she said. "Part of it is rumor, like the financial troubles with their real-estate development. Part of it has been confirmed. Once all of it is confirmed, we're going to run with it."

We sat eating our burgers and shakes on a bench on the large pier near the aquarium. To my left was a high suspension bridge, built so that navy ships could pass underneath.

"Run with it?" Mike repeated.

"Yes. A big documentary. I'm thinking a story this big might be my break. I might be able to go from regional news to national news." Her eyes glistened as she dreamed out loud. "Can you see me now on ABC or NBC?"

Her ambition was so obvious that I knew we'd be able to get information from her. As long as she thought it would help her get a bigger news story than the one she believed she already had.

"The morning that Ted Emmett was arrested at the country club," I said. "You were there, weren't you? Waiting as the police took him away."

She nodded.

"Someone gave you a tip, right?"

She nodded again.

"Didn't you think that was strange?" I asked.

"We get tips all the time."

"I mean, didn't you think it was strange that the police knew to arrest Ted Emmett so quickly? And that someone else knew the arrest was going to happen?"

She shrugged. "Never look a gift horse in the mouth."

"I've always wondered what that meant," Mike said. "I bet horses have bad breath."

"Mike," I sighed. "When people buy horses, they check the horses' teeth to see how old they are. If the horse is a gift, you don't need to worry about its condition, because you're not paying for it."

"I get it." His face wrinkled as he frowned. "But what if they were giving you that horse for a reason that helps them more than you?"

"Exactly!" I looked at the redheaded reporter. "Is there anyone you know that would be helped by Ted Emmett's arrest? His partner maybe, Thomas Stang?"

"Don't know why it would help Stang," she said. "They run a stockbroker business together. Whatever hurts the reputation of one of them also hurts the reputation of their business."

It was my turn to nod. "So aren't you curious why Stang called you with the second tip about Emmett's confession?"

She nibbled on her lower lip. It put some of her thick

lipstick on her front teeth. When she spoke, it was hard not to stare at the glob.

"Generally," she said, "something like that happens because the person calling it in wants to shape the way we report it. It's known as spinning the news in a favorable direction. With Thomas Stang, we didn't give him the chance."

"Did he try?" I asked.

"Like I said, we didn't give him the chance. We just moved right along with the story."

She didn't realize it, but her answers were very helpful. But we needed to know more.

"Can you tell me about the real-estate project?" I asked.

"It's a condominium project on the beach, about ten miles out of town. Built as second homes for people who live up north. The condominiums are very expensive. What we know for sure is that sales have been slow. The economy hit a downturn and too many of the condominiums have already been built but not sold. Which means that Ted Emmett and Thomas Stang owe the bank a lot of money, with not enough coming in right now to make payments."

"What if the condominiums sold?" Mike asked.

"Simple. The bank would be paid and the leftover money would be all profit. Lots of profit."

"They'll sell eventually?" I asked.

"Six months. A year. Maybe less, maybe longer. But until then, their reduced cash flow is almost enough to force them into bankruptcy."

We all fell into silence. Huge white pelicans flew down-river. They looked so graceful and magnificent in the air, flapping their wings occasionally and cruising in formation like a squadron of bomber planes.

"Maybe someone could lend them money," Mike said.

"With one of the partners in jail for confessing the museum theft? Not likely. They'll be lucky to keep half of their clients."

"Let me ask again," I said, "don't you think it's strange that Thomas Stang was willing to call you and give you a tip? I mean, if he was trying to spin the story, wouldn't he have called back?"

I could see doubt in her eyes. Just a little, but enough to make me press on.

"What if that's the real story?" I asked. "Thomas Stang."

"Impossible to prove."

"Maybe not if you found out a few answers for us."

Her eyes narrowed. "Answers? What kind of answers?"

I told her what we wanted. Just as I finished, her cell phone rang from her purse. She put up her hand to silence me as she lifted it out and answered. She listened intently, then said good-bye and put her cell back in her purse.

"I'll help," she told us. "Something is going on. Maybe it's what it appears, that Ted Emmett did go temporarily insane and steal the museum pieces. Or maybe there's something more behind it. Because . . ."

She nibbled her lip, as if she were debating whether to tell us.

"That was Stang again," she finally said. "With another tip. Later this afternoon, he's going to launch a lawsuit against Ted Emmett for destroying the reputation of their stockbroker firm."

CHAPTER 20

We finally had a chance to visit Mike's uncle Ted at three that afternoon. Although it had only been the morning of the day before that he'd been arrested, it seemed like it had happened a couple of weeks ago.

Mike and I took a taxi to the jail, leaving Ralphy and Lisa behind at the mansion that overlooked the water.

The jail cell was at the back of the police station; except for the officers in uniforms, the front of the station didn't seem any different than any regular office. It was the back half, however, that gave me shivers. There were about six holding cells on each side of a wide hallway. The thought of spending any time in those small concrete rooms was horrible. I couldn't imagine spending years inside.

I looked for Devon as we walked by the empty cells but didn't see him. We found out later that he was down at the courthouse, facing a judge as they arraigned him for a future trial date.

Theodore Emmett was in the final cell, still wearing the old-fashioned golf clothes that he'd been arrested in at the golf course.

He looked up at our approach and smiled, but it was a tired smile. I told myself that I was imagining things, that he didn't look about twenty years older than he had the day before.

"Good afternoon, gentlemen," he said. "Sorry to have spoiled your vacation."

After the guard left, Ted spoke cheerfully, as if trying to pretend we weren't in a jail cell with him.

"Well, boys, have you managed to find some fun things to do despite all of this?"

Mike and I glanced at each other. Since morning, we'd watched Devon get arrested, spied on Tom Stang, and met with a television reporter for a second lunch. I wasn't sure all of it could be defined as fun.

"Actually," Mike began, "we've been trying to figure a few things out."

Ted's mouth tightened in mild disapproval. "If you're referring to why I'm here, I wish you would just drop it."

I plunged ahead, knowing Mike would not want to offend his uncle.

"Sir," I said, "is it true that you and Mr. Stang took a major portion of your stockbroker's business and signed it over to the bank to be able to get a loan for a real-estate development that has accumulated some big debts?" This was something our redheaded reporter had also passed on to us.

"Please," he answered. "I really don't want to talk about it."

I spoke respectfully. "I just want to know that I understand this correctly. It's a beachfront condominium project about ten miles down the coast. It looks like all the condos will eventually sell, but in the short term, you and your partner, Tom Stang, have some big mortgage payments due within the next six months, and until the condos sell, you won't have the money to make the payments."

"Yes, yes," he said impatiently. "You've read what the newspapers have to say about this. That's what would lead a person to a desperate act, like stealing museum pieces."

"Pieces that you'd never be able to sell because they are unique and highly identifiable?" Mike asked.

Ted didn't reply.

"I think," Mike continued, "if you were going to steal something to make those payments, it would have been something much easier to sell. And I'm wondering if you would have spent all that money on our airplane tickets if you were so broke."

"Sir," I said, "we've also heard that you have arranged a trust fund for a local church and its charities. Some people would wonder why you did that if there wasn't any money."

"There isn't."

"And in six months?" I asked.

Ted looked at both of us and blinked. He looked down again. He had lost all of his fake cheerfulness.

"In six months," he finally said, quietly and slowly, "none of this will matter. Everything will be taken care of. Including your college education, Mike. Can you just trust me on this and stop asking questions?"

I wasn't sure what he meant by saying it would all be taken care of. But Mike and I did know something that might change Ted's confession.

"Sir," I said, "did you know that Tom Stang is about to send a lawyer here?"

Ted snorted. "My partner has been noticeably absent until now. His lawyer isn't going to do much good at this point."

"Uncle Ted, I don't think you're going to like why he's sending a lawyer. He's serving papers on you. A lawsuit."

We'd learned this from the reporter. Because Tom Stang had leaked it to her already.

"What!" The life came back into Ted's face with a sudden burst of anger.

"It's going to be on the news tonight. He is going to trigger a clause in your partnership agreement that allows him to purchase your half of the business at the value of the company right now."

"But . . . but . . ."

"The company is worth next to nothing?" I asked. "Especially with the mortgage payments due soon?"

"When the condos sell, it will be worth millions," Ted said. "In the meantime, I can assure you that in six months, those payments will be made in time to save the deal from collapsing."

"Except right now?" Mike asked. "What will it cost him to buy out your half right now when it looks like the deal will collapse?"

Ted's lack of response was enough answer. Then he straightened. "If I remember our partnership agreement, I also have the option of buying his half from him at the price he offers me. That's what I'll do."

"A shotgun clause," I said. "Isn't that what it's called? To make sure that in a buyout one partner offers a fair price to the other."

He frowned. "You know a lot more about this than I would expect."

Two hours earlier I hadn't known anything about this stuff. But then the reporter had called back with some answers.

"Sir, there's a small clause in your partnership agreement you might have forgotten. The morality clause. It states that because your reputations are so important in your stockbroker business . . ."

Ted buried his face in his hands and groaned.

I didn't have to finish. He knew the rest. If one partner did something criminal that would hurt the company's reputation, the other partner would have the option of purchasing the offending partner's half of the company at its current value as determined by an independent accounting firm.

"Either way," Ted said after he finished groaning,

"Tom Stang is able to buy out my half of the company. For next to nothing."

"Uncle Ted," Mike said, "does it now seem like Tom Stang would have every reason to be happy that those stolen museum pieces were found in the back of your car?"

"I guess. But—"

"But it also looks like Devon might be the one, doesn't it," I said quietly. "He worked at the museum. He would be an inside person able to find a way to steal things. And people know he has a record as a juvenile delinquent."

Ted shook his head slowly. "I'm the one who stole everything. That's my confession and that's how it will stand."

"Even if Tom Stang gets half your company for next to nothing?"

"Better than seeing Devon get accused of the theft."

"He wasn't driving your car that night," I said. "His girlfriend surprised him and took him to Savannah for an art festival. In her car."

"Devon wasn't driving the Mercedes?" Ted was already gray with exhaustion, but his face went a few shades paler.

"Her Mustang was fixed. They took that," I said.

"Which meant that someone else could have put the stolen pieces in the trunk of your car," Mike continued. "The same person who tipped off the police. And made sure you would be arrested in a highly public place. Then called the media."

"But . . . but . . ."

Mike spoke. "Did Tom Stang suggest and arrange for Devon's job at the museum?"

"Yes," Ted said after a brief pause. "As a matter of fact, he did. The director is one of Tom's clients."

"We know," I said. I pulled some folded sheets of paper out of my pocket. "Here's a printout of the information that Devon was looking for when he broke into your office this morning."

I handed the paper across to Ted. He unfolded it and glanced at it. Then he glanced at it again. Seconds later he was reading it carefully, as if Mike and I didn't even exist anymore.

Ted finished reading it a few minutes later. He spoke with new life in his voice.

"I now understand," he said. "This changes everything, doesn't it."

CHAPTER 21

It was midnight. I was on my stomach, hidden from Yankee soldiers who wanted to see me hanging by my neck from a rope. Strapped to my side was the legendary gilded saber, a sword that struck fear into the hearts of all soldiers who saw me. Above me was the bottom of a church pew, for that's where I was hidden.

On a rough wooden floor. Beneath the pews. In St. Michael's church. With cannonballs whistling overhead, bombarding the town in the ghostly light of a full moon that hung in a clear sky.

"Quit whispering to yourself," Lisa hissed beside me. "They could get here anytime."

So much for my little fantasy.

We *were* in St. Michael's church. We *were* beneath the pews, about five rows from the front.

But we weren't, of course, hiding from soldiers. And the whistling of cannonballs was simply my imagination as I remembered again the story about the high white steeple of St. Michael's rising from the darkness of the city and the Yankee cannon fire from Sumter Island.

Nor was it nighttime, but rather late afternoon, with thunderheads rising above Charleston. I could hear rising wind through one of the open church windows.

Then I heard the creaking of a door as it opened into the sanctuary of the church.

Then a set of footsteps.

Headed right toward us.

Then past us.

The footsteps stopped at a pew second from the front.

Then the owner of the footsteps settled in the pew and, unaware of a teddy bear taped to the underside of the pew bench beneath him, began reading a set of papers that Lisa and I had left there earlier.

We hardly dared breathe as we hoped and waited for a second set of footsteps.

Ted Emmett had thought all of this through for us. Half the reason he'd picked the church was because he knew the administrator, who cleared the use of the church for a meeting. Emmett had said he wanted a way to have proof that would stand up in court. That he needed Lisa and me as witnesses to the meeting.

Trouble was, it wouldn't be a meeting unless the second person showed up.

Five minutes later the door to the sanctuary opened again.

CHAPTER 22

"George?"

From our hiding place only three pews back, Lisa and I heard Tom Stang's voice clearly. That was the other half of the reason that Ted Emmett had picked the sanctuary of the church. Because it was far more quiet than a restaurant or any other public place.

This quiet and solitude was extremely important because we needed the conversation recorded. Hidden in the teddy bear was a voice-activated tape recorder. The only hope we had for proving Ted Emmett's innocence was a conversation between Tom Stang and George Reah, director of the Civil War museum. Lisa and I were here as backup witnesses, in case either man claimed in court that the tape had been made by a computer program that faked their voices.

Still, there would be no conversation unless George Reah was angry enough to talk. And that's why we'd set a small stack of papers on the pew. And followed Ted Emmett's instructions and made the anonymous phone call telling George to look in the church for them.

"Stang," George said back.

I smiled. George Reah had called Ted Emmett's partner by his last name, not his first. To me, that was a good indication that Reah *had* read through the papers.

"I'd like an explanation," Reah said. I heard a rustle of papers. George was probably waving the papers at Stang.

"So would I," Stang answered. "I told you I don't like people knowing we are connected beyond our stockbroker-client relationship."

"I'm not sure you're much of a stockbroker," Reah said, his voice growing more angry. "Especially after going through these papers."

On the floor, I could see the shoes and pants of the lower legs of both men. They stood near the second pew from the front. Near the voice-activated tape recorder.

So far, so good.

"What kind of papers?" Stang asked.

"Client reports. *Your* clients. Including some who made money on the same stocks that almost wiped me out."

"Where did you get those?"

"That matters far less than whether they are true and accurate." Reah had nearly begun to shout. "Stang, you recommended that I go short on the very same stocks you told all your other clients to go long on! It's as if you deliberately tried to drive me into bankruptcy!"

CHAPTER 23

This was what Ralphy had been able to finally figure out and what we'd brought to Ted Emmett. What the client list meant and why it was so important.

Most of the time, people enter the stock market by actually buying stocks. They pay their money at the beginning, then wait to see if their stocks go up or down in value, hopefully up. At the very worst, if a stock goes down to zero, they will lose all they have invested in that stock. But at least they'll never lose more than what they've already put into it.

There is another way of buying stocks, however. Much more risky. Basically, it's like gambling. You commit to buying shares at a certain price at a specific time in the future. If they are worth more than the agreed price at that time, you get a profit. But if they are worth less, you lose money because you have to make up the difference.

The most important thing is to guess right. Bet that the stock shares go "long," or up in value, and hope they go long. Or bet that they go "short," or down in value, and hope they go short.

The difference is very simple. When you buy shares outright, you can't lose any more money than what you put into them. When you gamble on whether a stock will go "long" and be worth more in the future, and it does the opposite and goes "short," then you can lose money you didn't have in the first place.

Which is exactly what happened to George Reah. To the tune of three hundred thousand dollars.

Which was why Reah had just accused Stang of deliberately trying to bankrupt him.

Money isn't the root of evil, as my dad once explained to me. Most people think that's what the Bible says. But the verse in 1 Timothy about money actually says that "the love of money" is the root of evil.

Dad had gone on to discuss it with me.

He said that the love of money leads some people to eighty-hour workweeks, constant and exhausting business trips, ulcers, and heart problems from stress as they sacrifice families and health for huge salaries. The love of money, he said, leads others to lie or cheat or betray friendships and integrity and, in the darker shadows of the criminal world, even to murder. He also pointed out that the love of money leads some of the fortunate and already wealthy to hoard their money when it is capable of doing so much good when shared.

Why is it so easy to love money?

I think it's because from the first time someone puts a quarter or a dollar into your hand when you're a kid and you get to choose your own candy at the store counter, you suddenly understand how much power money has. And it only gets worse as you grow older. Money gives you bicycles, then motorcycles, then cars.

In our world, everything has a price tag on it, and we learn very early to ask how much things cost.

I thought of what Thomas Stang had done to George Reah. I thought of George Reah's greed as he allowed Thomas Stang to talk him into going short and losing all that money.

It showed me that Dad was so right.

Instead of asking how much money something will cost us, we should ask a much more important question.

What price do we have to pay for money?

What price had George Reah paid for his?

CHAPTER 24

"Now, George, don't jump to conclusions," Tom Stang was saying. "Client reports are very tricky to read."

"I notice you didn't deny the charges. Look at this. Twenty of your clients made money by going short on the same stock where I went long. And, I might add, I went long on your advice. Are you telling me that the other twenty ignored your advice? Or did you give them different advice?"

"George, this is not the place to—"

"And look again. Fifteen of your clients made money by going long on the same stock where I went short. Again, it was your advice that I trusted. So did you give those fifteen clients the same advice but they ignored it? Or did you perhaps tell them to go long, while I was the only client you told to go short?"

"George—"

"Three hundred thousand dollars! You promised me I'd make money without spending money. That all I had to do was take your advice, and in a few months, I'd be rich. Instead, I wake up one morning to discover I'm going to lose everything if I don't come up with money I don't have. That I'm going to lose my house. My retirement funds. Even my car."

This was going far better than I could have hoped.

"You didn't lose anything, did you?" Tom said.

"No. Because you bailed me out. And at the time, I thought you were doing it because you were worried about me. But I know better now, don't I."

"George—"

"Simple, you said. Just make sure you can get into the museum. All you wanted was time alone at night for some historical research. Except all those pieces went missing. And by then I couldn't tell the police I was the one who'd let the thief into the museum, could I?"

"George, that problem is taken care of, too, isn't it? The thief was caught. In fact, he confessed."

"Are you telling me that you invited Ted Emmett into the museum that night?"

"I'm just saying," Tom Stang said smoothly, "that Emmett has confessed to the theft, the stolen pieces have been recovered, and you didn't lose any money in the stock market."

Stang paused. "So the big question is, how did you get those papers and why did you leave a message with my secretary to meet here of all places?"

"Me?" George Reah said, his anger now mixed with confusion. "I didn't leave a message with your secretary."

George wasn't lying. Ted Emmett had left the message.

George continued. "I only came here because some-body told me to come to the church and I'd find these papers."

"Who?" Stang demanded.

"Don't know."

"Someone sent you here," Stang said after a pause of only a second. "And someone sent me here. In other words, we were set up."

It became very quiet in the church sanctuary.

Then I saw Stang's feet move. And his hands and knees hit the floor.

He began to look around.

I was afraid he would see us. But his eyes were first attracted by the nearby teddy bear. The teddy bear that I had used to muffle any whirring sounds of the voice-activated tape recorder.

Stang snarled and ripped it loose.

He stood again.

"What's inside here?" he asked. "It looks like a tape recorder."

That's when I rolled over and stood and darted out of my pew toward him.

CHAPTER 25

My intent was to make a diving tackle, knock the teddy bear loose, grab it, and run. The only hope of proving Ted Emmett's innocence was on that tape. Ralphy had come up with the plan of putting the two of them together once we figured out the same thing about the client list that George Reah had just realized.

If we lost this tape now, however, there was no way they would fall for the same trick again. And since Ted Emmett had already confessed, there seemed no other way of proving that Stang had stolen the pieces and framed Emmett.

So I ran and dived.

Stang simply raised a fist and timed a perfect rabbit punch into the side of my head. He didn't have to swing hard. My momentum carried me into the punch and I hit the floor, flat on my back, just like he had dropped a piano on me.

I didn't even have a chance to groan before he stepped on my throat.

"You," he said. "I've seen you before."

I tried shifting sideways. He put pressure on my throat with his foot.

"Won't take much pressure to crush your windpipe," he said. "I'd stay put. And I'd tell me what's going on."

His eyes widened in recognition. "You're one of the kids that Ted Emmett invited for the golf tournament. A friend of his nephew."

He put a little more weight on his foot. It felt like my eyeballs were being squeezed from my head.

"Tell me," he said. "You're one of them, right?"

I said I was, but it came out as a gargle.

He eased off.

"Yes," I said.

"And this whole setup? You made it happen?"

I gargled again, as if the pressure of his foot was too much for me to speak.

He stepped on my hand with his other foot. He remained there, balanced with most of his weight on my hand and just enough on my throat that I couldn't move.

"You set this up," he repeated. "Right?"

Stang tossed the teddy bear to George Reah. "See what this is about while I make this kid talk."

My hand was in agony. My throat felt as if a boa constrictor was choking the life out of me. I couldn't think, couldn't come up with a way to keep Reah from turning the teddy bear over and finding a hole cut in the bear's belly where I'd hidden the tape recorder.

"Aarrggh," I said.

"A tape recorder," Reah said. He'd turned over the teddy bear and saw the plastic back of the recorder.

As he reached to pull it out, I was rescued by a book of hymns.

More accurately, a book of hymns thrown by Lisa.

With their attention on me, they must not have noticed her get into position. She'd taken one of the heavy books and thrown it sideways, like a Frisbee. The first one caught George Reah in the side of the head, and he dropped the teddy bear to clutch at his skull.

The front edge of the second one hit Tom Stang in the ear. He yelped and fell sideways, lifting his foot from my throat. I yanked my hand out from under his other foot, and that knocked him over completely. His head bonked the side of the pew, and he moaned as he staggered.

A third hymnal hit George Reah in the belly. He doubled over.

I flipped on my stomach and crawled forward, and a fourth hymnal bounced off my back.

I didn't care. The incoming hymnals were a great distraction.

I closed my hand over the teddy bear and bolted forward.

Hymnals kept crashing.

"Run," I shouted to Lisa. "Run!"

I dared to stand.

But as I turned, Tom Stang managed to block the aisle. I couldn't run past him to the safety of the outside of the church.

I turned toward a side door. Lisa slid out of the pew and headed in the same direction. We reached the door at the same time.

I pulled it open, expecting to see lawn and trees and sky.

Instead, there were stairs.

But it was too late to turn back. Tom Stang and George Reah had both recovered and were running toward us. They were too big for us to fight. So Lisa and I stepped inside and shut the door.

Just before Stang arrived, I managed to slide a bolt into place. But he hit the door hard and nearly popped the bolt loose. The door wasn't built to stop a determined pile driver.

Stang hit it again, probably with a shoulder. The door nearly broke off its hinges.

That meant we'd have to take the stairs.

"Up!" Lisa shouted.

Up it was.

Two steps at a time.

The door below us crashed open.

Lisa and I pounded upward. And then reached a dead end.

We'd climbed the steeple, and there was no place to go.

Heavy panting reached us as Stang and Reah pursued us.

"They've got no place to go," I heard Stang say. "Unless they want to jump."

He was right. I briefly wondered about trying to climb over, but the view from the top of the steeple made me dizzy.

At any other time, it would have been breathtaking. With the dark thunderclouds as a backdrop, all of old

Charleston was spread below us. The ancient buildings. The gardens and courtyards. The beautiful old houses. And the cemeteries.

Cemeteries.

That was where Lisa and I would be next if we tried to climb over or jump.

CHAPTER 26

Seconds later, Stang and Reah reached the top of the steps. They stopped just short of the platform where Lisa and I were trapped.

Both of them were puffing. Reah had a red welt on his cheekbone where the first hymnal had hit. Stang's hair was messed up, and he had a welt below his ear. George grabbed Lisa and twisted her arm behind her back so that she couldn't move.

"Give it to me, kid," Tom Stang snarled, pointing at the teddy bear.

I leaned over, holding the teddy bear above the ground far below. I waved as hard as I could.

"Help!" I managed to shout once.

Then Stang had me by the shoulder.

"Now!" Stang's voice was raspy with rage and heavy breathing from his run up the steps. "Or I throw you over with it."

Still I didn't let go.

"I'm not joking, kid," he continued. "All I'd have to do is lift you by the legs and shove you over."

"You'd kill me to protect your secret?"

"Give it to me."

"Why?" I asked. "Why frame Ted Emmett?"

"No games." He squeezed my shoulder hard. "Give it to me."

"I know you wanted to trigger the shotgun clause and buy out his half of the business. But why? It's almost bankrupt. All you would end up owning are debts."

He frowned, surprised. "How did you know that?"

I shrugged. "So it's true?"

"Whatever you think you know won't matter." An unpleasant smile crossed his face. "There's nothing you can prove."

"You've thought all of this through." The tape recorder was still active, and I wanted him to talk as much as possible. "You had easy access to the Mercedes. All you'd have to do is borrow Emmett's keys and get them copied. Reah here lets you into the museum, you take the pieces, put them in the Mercedes, then tip off the police to arrest Emmett in a highly public place to ruin his reputation even more."

"This is tiresome, kid. If you've got this taped, it won't matter, because I'll have the tape right away. Unless you want me to throw you from the top of this steeple along with it. I promise you, you'll be as broken as the tape recorder."

"What about the fire at Emmett's place? That was you. Devon wrestled with you and grabbed one of your cuff links. So he knew it was you starting the fire. Had you returned to the Mercedes to make sure nothing was in it?

And once he knew it was you, he decided to break into your office and look for evidence."

Irritation crossed Stang's face.

"Please shut your mouth. I'm going to count to five. If you don't give me the tape recorder by then, you're dead."

He moved beside me and reached for it. Briefly both our faces were over the edge. That was all I needed. His face. In plain sight to anyone down below.

I let go of the teddy bear.

He watched it fall with a smile of satisfaction.

"George, make sure these kids stay here while I go and retrieve the tape," he said.

"You got it," George answered. "But that's the last thing I'll ever do to help you."

"Except keep your mouth shut," Stang said. "You're in this as deep as I am. It will be their word against ours, and no one will believe them against the two of us."

Stang paused before heading down the steps. He grinned an evil grin at me.

"You lose, kid," he said.

This wasn't the moment to tell him he was wrong.

Because down below, waiting for him to step outside, were the redheaded reporter and her cameraman.

That was part of our deal with her. That she would be the first to get the story. With the tape recorder, with Lisa and me as witnesses, and with her cameraman hidden in a place to film Stang and Reah going in and coming out of the church, there would be no denying they had had the conversation recorded on the tape.

The tape recorder and the tape?

They were tucked in my waistband, beneath my shirt. Where I'd hidden them as Lisa and I ran up the stairs of the steeple. Where every word—including Stang's threats to kill me to protect his secret—was safely waiting for a judge and jury to hear.

CHAPTER 27

"You had confessed because you thought Devon was the thief, right? You thought he was driving the Mercedes the night the stuff was taken from the museum."

Mike was speaking to his uncle Ted. The three of us were in the courtyard behind the mansion while Lisa and Ralphy were getting doughnuts from a coffee shop on Broad Street. Ted had been released from jail the previous evening, shortly after Mike and I had brought the tape recording to the police station. Although he'd gone to bed really early, Ted's face was puffy and seemed as gray as ashes. As if he hadn't slept well.

"Yes, Mike," he answered. He stared at the ruins of the garage. It had finally stopped smoking. "With Devon's past, I knew he'd be the one they blamed. Especially since he worked there. And I didn't want the rest of his life ruined."

"But Devon broke into Stang's office to try to prove Stang was up to something," Mike said. "Because Devon knew your confession was going to ruin the rest of *your* life."

"Yes," Ted answered. He spoke with a sad tone. "All of the rest of my life."

"Wow," Mike said. "That's cool, actually. That you would be willing to do that for him."

"It would have been the least I could have done as a father, Michael. Because of how little I had done for him when it really mattered."

Ted took a deep breath. "I live in a big fancy house. I've made millions. But I paid a price for it. Eighty- or ninety-hour workweeks. I missed Devon's ball games. I missed his school plays. When he was a little boy, I wasn't there when he woke up in the morning. I wasn't there to say prayers with him when he went to sleep. And when my wife died . . ."

He closed his eyes briefly, as if the sadness was hitting him all over again. "When she died, I hired a nanny. I threw myself into work to forget about how sad I was. I started putting in even longer workweeks. For all practical purposes, Devon didn't have a father while he grew up. If I'd been there, I doubt he would have gotten into the serious trouble that he did."

"Samantha said about a year ago you guys started going to church together," I said. "He knew you cared then."

"Yup. About a year ago. We became friends. I slowed down at work. I realized what was important about life. And I wish I had longer to enjoy it."

"Uncle Ted," Mike said, "you make it sound like you're going to die any day now."

Ted smiled sadly. "I am."

I remembered something that Devon had said earlier when we'd asked him about insurance on the garage fire. *A lot of good insurance does a person who's going to die.*

I remembered what Ted had said barely a minute earlier. *Yes. All of the rest of my life.*

As if he didn't have much time left.

"Let me tell you guys something," Ted said. "And I hope you remember it as long as you live. Money and possessions mean nothing against the importance of your souls. I have everything a man could want. And even if I had billions, in the end, I would still die. So what is it worth? Nothing. The richest man in the world can't buy what matters. Love. And living life right. And making sure your soul is at peace with God. I didn't understand this until my doctor told me I have cancer. It's from all my years of smoking. You guys are smart to stay away from cigarettes."

He allowed himself a smile. "It was about a year ago. I'm lucky. It's given me time to realize the important things in life. I have only a few months left, but I was able to change. Spend time with Devon. Go back to church. Place my faith in God. I'm sad, of course, but grateful I didn't die suddenly before I had a chance to figure out what was important."

Another deep breath. "Like bringing you here. I wanted to meet you, Mike. You're my only nephew. It didn't matter to me how much your plane tickets cost. Or that it would cost more to pay for your friends. I've got much more than I can spend in this life anyway, and even if I was going to live for a long time, I'd want to spend it on others. In fact, Mike, I have arranged for a college scholarship for you."

"A scholarship!" Mike's face broke into a wide grin. Then he must have realized Ted Emmett had made the arrangements because cancer had changed his life and his attitude. Mike's grin faded some.

Ted continued. "And scholarships for your friends, Ricky and Lisa and Ralph. That wasn't my original plan, but without them, I would have lost my entire business and my reputation and any chance to provide for Devon after my death."

Ted smiled at me. "So, thanks."

I didn't know what to say. Here was a man who knew he was going to die any day. *Should I tell him I'm sorry? Or that I'm glad I get a scholarship?*

Ted saved me the difficulty. "Both of you. Cheer up. I'm all right with what lies ahead. We all have to die, you know. Sometimes I think living is about learning to die well. And I've been given that chance."

I nodded slowly.

"Sir?"

"Yes, Ricky."

"I don't understand. Your real-estate development. Everyone says it's in trouble."

"It is."

He grinned at my confusion. "Short term, it's in big trouble. There are some huge payments due in about six months, and we haven't sold enough properties to cover those payments. But long term, it's in great shape, because it's a good investment and when the economy turns around, people will buy those properties."

"But the short-term payments," Mike said. "I thought if you didn't make them that . . ."

"Yes. I lose it all. Correction, my corporation loses it all. But you see, when Thomas and I went into the development, we took out what is called keyman life insurance. His death or mine would pay out all the mortgages because the bank is listed as the beneficiary. For him, my death was the perfect solution to our troubles. But he wanted more than just his half. Because a few months ago, I told him about my cancer."

It hit me.

"I think I understand," I said. "The business is worth next to nothing right now because of your debts. So Stang set all of this up to buy your half with hardly any money. He knew as soon as you died, the life insurance policy would make the business worth a lot more."

"About ten million dollars more. You see, once the life insurance policy is in place, the keyman insurance pays out the mortgage even if I'm no longer owner. The policy was set up so that the beneficiary could not be changed."

"Wow," Mike said.

"Wow," I said.

"And you know what's funny?" Ted asked.

I wasn't sure I could see anything funny about this.

"Now I get to buy the business off him at next to nothing. I can trigger the shotgun clause. And because he broke into the museum and did all that he did, he also broke the morality clause. His half of the business will become mine.

When I die, the insurance will still pay out. I'll be able to set up even more charities and trust funds with all those millions."

Mike and I didn't have a chance to reply.

Lisa and Ralphy walked into the courtyard with a box of doughnuts.

"Hey," Lisa said. "You're not going to believe the ridiculous thing that Ralphy tried to tell me about the history of Charleston and what Yankee soldiers shot from cannons."

Mike stood. "I think I'll go get some glasses and milk for our doughnuts."

"No," Lisa said. "Stay. That way you can explain to Ralphy where you got the crazy idea that the soldiers chopped up dead elephants and fired cooked meat at people."

I stood. "That's right, Michael. You explain. *I'll* get the milk."

Epilogue

A week later, the four of us were back in Jamesville. I had met up with Ralphy and Mike in Mike's backyard, where the Andrews family had a swimming pool.

"Hot," Mike said. He stood and stretched unnecessarily. The sun was baking us like we were steaks on a grill.

"Yup," I said from a lawn chair. I tilted back a can of soda and sucked out the last few drops. I waved in Mike's direction. "As host, shouldn't you be looking for more of this?"

Ralphy was nearby, dipping a toe into the water. Hot as it was, he hated the shock of the cold water. Ralphy always preferred to ease his way into the pool.

"Sure," Mike said. "Just let me make a quick detour."

He stepped in Ralphy's direction and shoved him into the pool. Ralphy landed headfirst and came up sputtering and yelling.

Mike grinned. "Be right back."

As Ralphy dog-paddled in the water, Mike moved to the back door.

"Hey, who locked it?"

I didn't answer, because Mike was already at the window of the kitchen that overlooked the backyard. "Mom!" he shouted. "Mom!"

Mike came back to us.

"She said she had to do some shopping. She's got a habit of locking all the doors when she leaves."

"I'm thirsty," I said.

"And I'm going to get you back," Ralphy said. "Somehow, sometime."

"Right," Mike snorted. "In the meantime, I'll get some sodas."

"Door's locked," I said in a helpful voice.

"Doggie door isn't."

Mike pointed at the pet door with a flap. "Last summer I got in and out all the time through there."

"Mike . . ."

Too late. He was already moving.

Ralphy stayed in the pool, his hair slicked back and wet. I rubbed some sunscreen on my chest.

Mike began to crawl through the pet flap.

"Hey!" he yelled. But his voice was muffled because his head and shoulders were already through the pet door.

"Be funny if he got stuck," I said to Ralphy. "Be pretty easy for you to figure out a way to get him back."

"Hey!" Mike yelled again. "I'm stuck."

I wandered over and talked to the back end of his bright orange swimming trunks. "Stuck?"

"No kidding, Einstein."

"Thought you did this all the time."

"That was last summer." He grunted as he tried to wiggle loose. But his shoulders were through the opening and he couldn't back out. And his hips were too wide. "I don't understand. I must have grown since last summer."

"Great," I said. "Now it looks like I'm going to have to go to the store to get some soda."

"No!" he yelped. "You've got to do something."

The phone rang. It was a cordless phone, back at the lawn chairs.

"Be glad to help," I said. "I'll answer the phone."

"Hey!" Mike yelled again. "Come back here!"

"Hello?" I said. "Andrews residence."

I recognized the voice right away. "Devon! Good to hear from you. Everything going great?"

"You bet," he answered from Charleston. "Any chance of speaking to Mike?"

I swiveled. Mike had made no progress. From this end, all we could see were his bright orange swimming trunks and his legs, kicking slightly.

"He might have to call you back," I answered Devon.

"I'm just stepping out," he said. "Could you give him some news and tell him to call me tonight?"

"Sure."

Devon spoke and I listened for a few minutes. Then I said good-bye and hung up.

I wandered over to Mike.

"How you doing?" I asked.

"Very funny," his muffled voice answered. "I'm still stuck."

I told him that Devon had just called.

"He's got great news," I explained. "Your uncle Ted is doing much better. The doctors think that since he's a lot less stressed out now, his body is able to fight the cancer better."

"Good," Mike said.

"And Devon and Samantha are engaged," I continued. "He proposed to her last night."

"Yuck," Mike said.

"They want all of us to go back out to Charleston for the wedding," I finished. "Probably around Christmas-time."

I pushed Mike a little with my foot. "Of course, you might still be stuck in the door by then."

"Very funny," he said.

Ralphy reached me, dripping wet from the pool. Some of the water fell on Mike's back.

"Hey!" Mike yelled. "Cut that out!"

I grinned at Ralphy. I pointed at the nearby garden hose and made a motion with my hand for him to turn it on and spray Mike.

"Come on," Mike pleaded. "Do something."

Ralphy was already running for the hose.

"Sure," I said. "We'll do something. Right away."